Buzzer Basket

The Chip Hilton Sports Series

For more information on
Coach Clair Bee and **Chip Hilton**
please visit us at
www.chiphilton.com

Chip Hilton Sports Series
#20

Buzzer Basket

Coach Clair Bee
Foreword by Bob Hammel,
Author and Sportswriter

Updated by Randall and Cynthia Bee Farley

BROADMAN
&HOLMAN
PUBLISHERS

Nashville, Tennessee

0-8054-2099-1

Published by Broadman & Holman Publishers,
Nashville, Tennessee

Subject Heading: BASKETBALL—FICTION / YOUTH
Library of Congress Card Catalog Number: 2001035497

Library of Congress Cataloging-in-Publication Data
Bee, Clair, 1900–83
    Buzzer basket / Clair Bee ; updated by Randall and
Cynthia Bee Farley ; foreword by Bob Hammel.
        p.   cm. — (Chip Hilton sports series ; #20)
    Summary: Chip faces difficult challenges in dealing with
a new basketball coach and increased responsibilities at
Mr. Grayson's store.
    ISBN 0-8054-2099-1 (pb)
    [1. Basketball—Fiction. 2. Universities and colleges—Fiction.]
I. Farley, Randall K., 1952– . II. Farley, Cynthia Bee, 1952– .
III. Title.

P27.B38196Bu   2001
[Fic]—dc21   2001035497

1 2 3 4 5 6 7 8 9 10 05 04 03 02 01

"Al"
(Albert Francis Quin)
treasured friend

COACH CLAIR BEE, 1962

Bob Hammel and Tom Geyer
Both of whom know
the meaning of loyalty

RANDY AND CINDY FARLEY, 2001

Contents

Foreword

AS A ROOKIE FATHER, I made what I thought was a prudent move as my son reached the point in school when book reports were expected of him.

No sports books, I said.

This was a career sportswriter talking. This was a father who knew son Rick had been exposed to far more than his share of sports reading. Make the kid branch out, my inner self said.

Then I got to thinking.

When I was a boy, I developed an insatiable appetite for reading precisely because I read things I wanted to read. Yes, that did include some sports books but also biographies and boys' action books—all sorts of things that met no particular criterion except I really wanted to read them.

The main objective, I concluded, was nurturing a fondness for reading that would stick for life and guarantee an educational regeneration that never would end.

And I also thought of Chip Hilton.

I came along just a bit too early for Chip. About eight years apparently. That was the age difference between my younger brother Jim and me. I watched Jim get all caught up in Chip's derring-do. Birthdays and Christmas were never a gift problem where Jim was involved. If there was a new Chip Hilton book out, if there was one he somehow had missed in the past, it was perfect. One Christmas, out of curiosity, I took the time to read one before I wrapped it. The kid brother has good taste, I decided. And I always "preread" them after that.

Jim became an athlete, a pretty good one. Then a coach, a very good one. Then a father, his first child named James Robert.

And, from the crib on, that first child was called Chip. Still is.

That's just part of the reason I'm happy to see the Chip Hilton series come back.

The other is that I was lucky enough to meet the author.

My background in sportswriting introduced me to Coach Clair Bee before I knew he had any connection with Chip Hilton and before my brother Jim knew Chip Hilton had any connection with one of the greatest coaches—basketball, football, any kind of coaches—who ever lived.

I knew Coach Bee was a pioneer of the sport all Hoosiers love. I knew he had much to do with shaping the way the game was played. I knew that when New York was the capital of college basketball, he was a primary reason— he and Joe Lapchick and Nat Holman, three giants of the early game.

What I didn't know I was educated about later because one of the giants of the later game, Coach Bob Knight, came to Bloomington in 1971 to coach the Hoosiers. As a sports-writer for the hometown newspaper, I was able to observe the special relationship between Knight, Bee, and the sport of basketball.

Coach Bee had no greater fan than Bob, who revered him in both roles—author and coach. Knight loved to have Coach Bee watch and critique his Indiana University team. In 1976, he asked wiry little Clair Bee—eighteen days after his eightieth birthday—to speak to the players in the locker room before the NCAA Mideast Regional Championship game.

Five years later, blind by then from glaucoma, Coach Bee was brought to Bloomington to be around another championship-bound Indiana team. That team's leader was Isiah Thomas, separated in age from Bee by three generations. Thomas was captivated by the energy, the enthusiasm, the animation of the little cricket who kept a whole team wide-eyed as he talked to them of their opportunities and obligations as kids fortunate enough to play at college basketball's highest level.

Two years later, Clair Bee died. To Bob Knight, Isiah Thomas, and the Indiana players in those two locker rooms, he never will die.

And now, with the renewal of the Chip Hilton Sports series, there's a good chance that Chip Hilton never will either.

You have to like a world like that.

Bob Hammel
Author and Sportswriter

CHAPTER 1

Three-Time
All-American

VALLEY FALLS'S basketball captain, the best high-school
player in the state, dribbled upcourt. He trapped the ball
first with his left hand and then with his right. And all the
time he watched the clock and faked with the ball and his
feet. He feinted with his head, eyes, and shoulders in one
last desperate attempt to catch his guard off balance. The
one-on-one was the captain's favorite play, and his teammates had cut to the other side of the court to give him room
to operate.

But nothing worked. His relentless alumni opponent had
leeched him every second and had stopped him cold. Now,
with the score tied 86-86 and the clock running out, the
high-school star had a chance to win the game. He felt it
would make up for all his previous failures to win against
this opponent.

On any other night, Valley Falls's fans would have concentrated on the high-school captain's tantalizing fakes and
feints to outwit his opponent before driving in for the score.
But not this game! Tonight was the homecoming game, a

contest that pitted the current varsity basketball team against Valley Falls's alumni. But tonight the fans were watching Chip Hilton. In fact, they had watched every move the college star made on the bench and on the court!

The blond defensive player crouched in a wrestler's stance with one long arm reaching forward toward the ball and the other extending wide to his side. He looked straight ahead. His face appeared expressionless, but his alert gray eyes seemed to encompass every player and every nuance of action on the court. The two opponents were about the same height, but Chip's broad, sloping shoulders and long arms and legs made him appear inches taller.

Suddenly, the high-school star made his move. He faked right, tapped the ball swiftly to the left, and started a hard drive. For a split second it looked as if he were on his way. Then, almost too fast for the eye to detect, Chip Hilton's right hand snaked forward and deflected the ball. The first jab was followed by a second that brought the ball under control. The alumni player expertly pivoted around the cha-grined dribbler and was halfway to his team's basket before the young high-school player could recover his balance and change direction.

Chip Hilton's long strides ate up the distance! He was far ahead of his pursuer when he dribbled under his basket. Without breaking stride, Chip rose high in the air and dunked the ball down through the net to give the alumni team a two-point lead. A tremendous cheer followed the play, but Chip appeared oblivious to the shouts and cheers of approval. He backtracked swiftly to a defensive position at midcourt and waited for his opponent to approach.

The clock showed twenty seconds left to play with the Valley Falls alumni leading 88-86. The high school players advanced the ball swiftly to their front court. Although closely guarded by his opponent, the captain called for the ball and attempted a desperate three-point shot far out on the side of the court for the win.

The lithe alumni player turned as the ball rimmed the hoop, boxed out his opponent with a swift pivot toward the basket, and then leaped high in the air for the rebound. Twisting his body while still in the air, Chip fired the ball out to the left sideline and into the hands of a redheaded teammate, Soapy Smith. It was perfect rebound technique, and the fans gave the alumni team another round of applause.

The gym was a bedlam of shouts and yells as Soapy pivoted rapidly and sped up the right sideline. While the fans were still applauding the play, the redhead passed the ball to a teammate breaking into the middle of the court. The middle man dribbled swiftly upcourt and then hit Chip with a chest-high pass just as he cut under the basket. The speedy college player went high in the air and laid the ball softly against the backboard to make the score 90-86 just as the buzzer ended the game.

Cheers of approval boomed once again, filling the high school gym. The enthusiasm continued as the players on both teams—all Valley Falls neighbors—shook hands and walked together off the court. They parted only after reaching separate locker room doors at the far end of the court. The alumni team was about to swing through the locker room door labeled "Visitors" when Chip smiled to himself. He had played in a homecoming game before, but it still felt strange going into this "other" locker room in his old high school gym.

Some spectators attempted to thread a path through the crowd, but they found it an impossible task. The fans were standing in the aisles and on the bleacher seats shoulder to shoulder, with scarcely enough room to permit a deep breath.

Despite the discomfort, nothing could have kept Valley Falls's basketball faithful from this game! This was the big night of the holiday season, the feature of Christmas week, the night of the annual homecoming alumni basketball game and dance.

The fans had enjoyed the game, but Chip Hilton, State's all-American star and the leading point scorer in the nation, was a product of Valley Falls. He was their hometown boy, and he provided the big thrill of the evening.

High in the stands, in the very last row of seats, two of Valley Falls's most prominent citizens were wedged in among the exuberant fans. Both men were now in their seventies, but they had enjoyed every minute of the action. John Schroeder owned The Sugar Bowl, the biggest pharmacy and soda shop in town, and Doc Jones was the most popular physician in the county.

"Just like his father," Doc Jones said, reminiscing. "Chip looks just like his dad did all those long years ago—same blond hair and gray eyes and lanky body."

"Chip's a better athlete than his father!" Schroeder said succinctly.

"Maybe," Jones drawled. "Anyway, not many doctors bring a father *and* his son into the world and live to see them both make all-American."

"That's for sure, Doc," Schroeder said thoughtfully. "Where do the years go? I can remember as if it were yesterday the day little Chip came to see me for a job. It wasn't long after his father was killed up at the pottery. And what a worker that young boy turned out to be—"

"Runs in the family," Jones interrupted. "Now take Mary Hilton. She works every day at the phone company. Never misses!" His eyes traveled around the rows of faces, and he shook his head. "I don't think she's here."

"She never was too keen on watching little Chip play. It brought back too many memories of Big Chip, I guess," Doc Jones replied.

There was a short silence between the two friends, and then Schroeder continued the conversation. "We've got a lot to be proud of in this little old town, Doc," he said slowly. "Our kids do well in college, and those who don't go away to school turn out to be first-class citizens. Yep, Valley Falls is all right."

"The State University athletic department must think so," Doc said crisply. "Chip and Soapy Smith and Speed Morris are on their basketball team. They beat our high-school kids almost by themselves tonight, and they only played half the game."

"Biggie Cohen and Red Schwartz aren't much in basketball," Schroeder observed, "but they did all right in football."

"So did Chip!" Jones said quickly. "How many sophomore football players can make all-American?"

"Not many," Schroeder observed. "As far as that goes, how many small towns like ours ever had five of their kids on the same college baseball team all at the same time? That's pretty impressive!"

"Don't forget it was Chip who pitched 'em to the national championship," Jones added significantly.

"How about those five kids," Schroeder mused aloud. "You might think they were brothers. They play four years of high-school baseball and football together, and now they're doing the same thing in college."

"Don't forget Hank," Jones said, gesturing toward the coach standing in front of the alumni bench. "He's been with them all the way."

"Biggest mistake the school board ever made," Schroeder said glumly. "They shouldn't have ever retired Hank Rockwell. Look at him! He's standing straight as a ramrod and in perfect health."

"Yeah," Jones said in admiration. "He's rough and tough and just as active as he was thirty years ago. All man!"

"State University picked him up fast enough," Schroeder said dryly. "They tell me every coach on the staff up there looks to him for advice."

"Wonder why they didn't give him the basketball job?" Jones asked.

"Hank didn't want it."

"I still can't understand why Corrigan left in the middle of the season," Jones grumbled. "It wasn't fair to the school . . . *nor* the players."

"Now, Doc," Schroeder said soothingly, "you know as well as I do that Corrigan got a Rhodes Scholarship."

"Sure! I know that. More power to him. Great! But why start the season?"

"You read the papers the same as I did," Schroeder chided.

"So?"

"So Corrigan didn't expect to go to England until next fall, but they said he could save a year by starting in February. He didn't hear about it until after the season had already started."

"I still don't think it was necessary, and I just don't like it. This would have been State's big year."

"*Would* have been!" Schroeder echoed. "What makes you think it still won't be?"

"A new coach for one thing. A rank beginner."

"Mike Stone is no beginner, Doc," John Schroeder replied, shaking his head. "No, he's been assistant coach at Northern State for six or seven years."

"*Was* assistant coach," Doc Jones corrected. "He got demoted."

"What do you—"

Doc Jones and John Schroeder were longtime friends, and like many people who spend a great deal of time together, they often anticipated each other's comments. Doc knew exactly what Schroeder was about to ask even before he finished asking.

"What I *know* is that Coach Brannon made his son varsity assistant and cut Stone's responsibilities way back. Stone used to do a lot of recruiting, but Brannon's son took that over too. The way I understand it, Stone and Brannon just didn't see things the same way. That's why State got him. Anyway, what's so great about Northern State?" Doc Jones challenged.

"It's simple enough, Doc. Northern State wins games! They've got the winning habit. They won the national championship a couple of years ago, and they're always one of the top teams in the country."

"What's that got to do with Stone?"

"Plenty!" Schroeder said quickly. "Mike Stone played three years at Northern State. He even made all-American. Besides, he knows their system inside and out."

There was a brief pause in the conversation, and then Schroeder grinned and playfully elbowed his friend in the ribs. "By the way, Doc, weren't you telling me the other day that players make the coach?"

"Sure! Why?"

"Well, State's got its best material in years. That seven-footer Chip dug up was just what the team needed. With him and Chip and Speed Morris and that dribbling magician . . . what's his name?"

"Chung. Jimmy Chung."

"Well, with those four and Dom Di Santis, State's got a good team. Maybe a great team! You saw what the kids did in Madison Square Garden in New York during the Holiday Invitational."

"They didn't win it," Doc grunted.

"No, but they went to the quarterfinals and landed in the consolation game. They could have won the whole thing if that big seven-foot junior had played ball in his sophomore year. Mark my words, Doc, State will win the national championship."

"They still need a coach," Doc persisted.

Schroeder grunted and changed the subject. "By the way, Mary Hilton came into the store the other day after work and said Chip's on the dean's list. How's that for a kid who plays three sports and works part time too? Pretty good, eh?"

"Just what you'd expect from Chip Hilton," Jones said softly. "But don't forget that Soapy Smith. He's doing the same thing."

"Not quite," Schroeder corrected. "Smith is working and playing ball, but he isn't on the dean's list—"

"Well, Soapy may not be on the dean's list," Jones said with a chuckle, "but that redheaded rascal will get along. He sticks with Chip like his shadow. If all it takes is studying to keep him with Chip, well, it's as good as done."

Schroeder nodded his agreement. "That's right. You see one of those kids, you see the other. What are they now, sophomores?"

Doc Jones shook his head. "Juniors."

"Can't be!"

"They are," Jones affirmed. "Chip made all-American in football as a sophomore and this past fall as a junior. Remember?"

"That's right," Schroeder said, nodding reflectively. "He made all-American in basketball too."

"He'll make it again this year," Jones said firmly. "And with another year to go, he'll be a three-time all-American player in three sports as sure as you're born. That's got to be some sort of a record in college athletics."

CHAPTER 2

A Game Worth Playing

CHIP HILTON had been surrounded almost as soon as he scored the game-ending basket. He was mobbed by his alumni teammates, college friends, neighbors, and admiring boys and girls who thrust game programs, pieces of paper, books, and pens and pencils toward him with pleas for autographs. It was embarrassing to be the center of so much attention, but Chip signed his name and exchanged greetings with all of them, his heart filled with pride. The attention made him feel conspicuous, but he also appreciated it.

Chip and Soapy Smith, his college roommate and best friend, walked slowly along with the high school players until they reached the corridor leading to separate locker rooms. But just as he was about to swing through the door, the high-school players crowded around him once again.

"Man, you rocked! It was great to play against you, Chip," the captain said, extending his hand. "I learned a lot!"

Chip gripped the teenager's hand firmly. "Thanks," he said warmly. "You gave me a *real* workout."

"Who's kidding who?" the captain grinned ruefully. "So real you got thirty points! That's not important though," he added hastily. "I got a chance to play against you. I'll remember that a *long* time."

"I'll remember it too," Chip countered. "By the way, I hope some of you guys are planning to go to State."

"We sure are!" the captain said quickly. "We're applying there, but we don't know if we'll make the team."

"You never know until you try," Chip countered.

"We're glad you played for keeps," one of the players said thoughtfully. "Lots of times the college players let up on us and let us win."

"That's right," another boy agreed. "They practically give us the game."

"But we don't want to win that way," the captain added.

"And we wouldn't want to lose that way," Soapy Smith said quickly, grinning broadly.

Chip's chest swelled with a feeling of pride as he glanced around the circle of teenage faces. These kids knew what sports is all about! An athlete plays with all he has and he plays for keeps. *All* the time.

"We've won five games in a row," one of the boys ventured.

"That's great!" Chip said warmly. "When it comes to winning or losing, Robert Kennedy, one of our United States attorney generals, said it best: 'A game worth playing is a game worth winning.' That just about sums up how an athlete should feel, whether he's playing during practice or a season championship."

The younger players nodded in agreement, and Chip and Soapy again shook hands with each of them before swinging through the doors of the visitors' locker room. They were just dropping down on the bench in front of the lockers when Coach Henry Rockwell walked through the door with the Valley Falls High School coach, the principal, and several of their former teachers. After visiting a short time, the crowd thinned out, and Coach Rockwell walked over beside Chip.

"Nice going, Chipper," the veteran coach praised, placing an arm over Chip's shoulders. "You put on a good show. See you tomorrow. Oh! I nearly forgot!"

He reached into the inside pocket of his wrinkled blue sports coat and pulled out a folded sheet of computer paper. "You had an E-mail message at home—your mom printed it out and sent your neighbor, Taps Browning, over with it right before the game. There was so much excitement around here that I forgot all about it. Sorry."

"That's all right, Coach," Chip said, opening the paper. Then, with Soapy peering over his shoulder, he read the message.

> January 2
>
> Hi Chip,
>
> I hate to disturb your holiday, but Mr. Grayson is seriously ill, and Mrs. Grayson would like you to return as soon as possible. She needs your help at the store.
>
> Thanks, Chip!
> Mitzi Savrill

"Oh, no!" Chip muttered, looking quickly at Soapy.

"He must be pretty sick," Soapy worried. "Mitzi wouldn't send for you if it wasn't serious. What are you going to do?"

"Head out right away!" Chip said quickly.

"I'm going too!" Soapy said emphatically. "I know! I'll drive! We can take the car my parents helped me buy! I told them I probably won't drive it much around University, but my parents, especially Mom, wanted me to have wheels. She said it might encourage me to come home more often. I figure it's just that Dad's tired of picking me up all the time. And then—"

Chip grinned and held up his hand to stem Soapy's barrage. "But there's no point in your going back early, too,

Soapy. I can take the train. School doesn't start until Wednesday."

"I know that," Soapy said grimly.

Chip smiled and tapped the E-mail message. "It wouldn't be because Mitzi sent this message, would it?"

"Huh!" Soapy grunted disdainfully, shrugging his shoulders. "Of course not!"

"No," Chip echoed. "Of *course* not."

"Honest!" Soapy said, evading Chip's eyes. Then a slow burn flooded his freckled face, and he grinned in defeat. "All right!" he conceded, his blue eyes brightening. "Maybe Mitzi's got a *little* to do with it."

"I thought so."

"It's mostly because of Mr. Grayson though," Soapy added seriously. "He's a great man, and he's been awfully good to us."

"You're right about that," Chip agreed quietly.

"Besides," Soapy continued, "it wouldn't be much fun if you weren't here. I've been running my parents ragged the last three days anyway. Dad said he and Mom would have to take a vacation as soon as I left."

"All right!" Chip said decisively. "We'll leave tonight."

Two hours later the two friends were heading down the highway on their way to University in Soapy's new car. Soapy sang along to the CD player, but Chip simply gazed out the window. The parade of glistening poles and wires and fences and snow-covered fields flew endlessly past the window. There was a bright moon, and the white landscape was broken from time to time by the dark silhouette of woods and villages with their white rooftops and dimly lighted streets.

The little towns dotting the way reminded Chip of Valley Falls. A sharp feeling of homesickness gripped him so that he wished he could be back in high school and working in John Schroeder's Sugar Bowl. He missed his mom already. He had always been amazed by her steadfast courage and gentle understanding. He was filled with such a great love for her that, for a moment, it threatened to overwhelm him. His father had died a number of years before, and Chip and his mother were very close. He always found it hard to leave her after school holidays.

Then he thrust the nostalgic thoughts aside. His mother was in good health and happy and getting along fine. *His* job right now was to get an education.

It seemed to Chip that he had just dozed off when Soapy jabbed him in the arm. "Wake up, Chipper. We're home. Good old Jefferson Hall!"

The two friends unloaded the car, carrying their gear up the broad, sweeping porch steps of the four-story brick residence hall and then up one more flight of stairs to room 212, their college home for the past two and a half school years.

Chip unlocked the door, and Soapy followed him in, dropping his duffel bag and backpack with two soft thuds. "Man! It's cold in here! They must turn the heat way down during vacation," he grumbled. "Well, anyway, I'm going to sleep." Soapy yawned widely, stretching from his toes to his outstretched fingers. "Mom said I wasn't getting enough sleep at home. You?"

Chip wasn't sleepy anymore, but he nodded anyway. The redhead wasted no time. He slipped swiftly into his red, white, and blue State University sweats, brushed his teeth, dove into his bed, ducked his head under a blanket, and said good night.

A few minutes later, Chip turned off the light and bundled up under his quilt. Soapy's references to his father that night had turned Chip's thoughts once more to home. Chip thought about his father. Big Chip, as he had been called, had made sports history at State University and had given Chip a good start in athletics. But he hadn't lived to enjoy the fruits of his coaching because of a fatal accident at the Valley Falls Pottery where he worked. Big Chip had saved the life of a careless workman but lost his own.

Chip's thoughts shot on ahead to University and his employer. George Grayson owned the largest drugstore in University, along with the soda shop and several other departments located in the big building.

George Grayson is a lot like a father, Chip reflected, *to a lot of us. . . .* And when it came to getting the best out of an employee, he was a lot like Coach Rockwell. He was strict and wanted a job done right, but he never rode anyone. He told his employees what he wanted done and then left them alone unless they ran into trouble.

Years ago, George Grayson had worked his way through State University, and Chip figured that was the reason his employer gave jobs to so many students. First, there was Mitzi. Mitzi Savrill had grown up in the town of University and was a student at State, but she had started working for George Grayson when she was just a sophomore in high school. She was now in charge of the books and was the store's chief cashier. Then there was the fountain crew, which included Soapy, Philip Whittemore, and Fireball Finley—all athletes. And on the other side of the large store, there were half a dozen pharmacy school students who were part-time employees.

Chip was thinking just then that he had the best job of everyone. He was in full charge of the stockroom, and every item that was sold at Grayson's in any of the departments had to go through his hands and through his computerized records. It was a tough assignment, but he really liked it. He reviewed his responsibilities. In addition to checking all incoming shipments and maintaining an accurate inventory, he and his assistant, Skip Miller, were also responsible for filling orders and delivering stock to the various departments in the store. George Grayson's accountant had installed an internal check system that was a big help with that task.

He grinned to himself as he thought about Skip Miller. The high school senior could have passed for Chip's younger brother. Skip was nearly as tall as Chip, and they both had gray eyes and short blond hair. Strangers almost always thought they were brothers. Skip was one of the best high-school athletes Chip had ever known, but his early success hadn't changed the young player's view of himself. He remained modest and quiet and a hard worker. And, Chip mused, a loyal friend.

This set him off on another tangent. An old axiom he had once read said that through an entire lifetime a person could count his true friends on the fingers of one hand. That might ring true for some people, but it sure didn't apply to him. There were Soapy, Speed, Biggie, Red, Fireball, Whitty, Henry Rockwell, George Grayson, Mitzi Savrill, Pete Thorpe, and Skip. In Valley Falls there were John Schroeder and Doc Jones, and that made thirteen total. There were more, too, if he counted players and coaches on the team such as Jimmy Chung and Branch Phillips and Coach Corrigan.

Chip was thinking that a person could make friends almost anywhere if he worked at it. The most important thing was to *be* a friend. He wondered whether Mike Stone, the new coach, would turn out to be a friend like Henry Rockwell and Jim Corrigan.

The next morning after breakfast at the student union, Chip and Soapy jogged downtown. They paused when they came to the corner of Main and Tenth streets and peered through Grayson's big plate-glass windows. The store was crowded with customers. They were jammed in the aisles between the showcases and three deep in front of the old-fashioned soda fountain. Mitzi Savrill was seated at the cashier's desk near the entrance.

"It's nine o'clock on a Tuesday morning!" Soapy said incredulously, stuffing his hands into his warm-up jacket. "What gives? Why are all these people here?"

"Inventory sale," Chip said succinctly. He led the way through the door and stopped in front of the cashier's desk.

Mitzi finished making change for a customer and then glanced up in surprise. "Chip! Soapy! When did you get back?"

"Late last night," Chip said.

"*I* wanted to see you first thing," Soapy said breezily.

"That's nice, Soapy," Mitzi said, smiling. Then her smile vanished and she breathed a sigh of relief. "I'm glad you're here, Chip. Mrs. Grayson asked me to bring you out to the house as soon as you arrived."

"What's the matter with the boss?" Soapy queried.

"I really don't know, Soapy. I *do* know that he worked day and night in the stockroom and even behind the fountain while you and Chip were playing basketball—"

Mitzi paused and hastily covered her mouth with her hand. "Oh! I didn't mean to say that! Anyway," she continued nervously, "we had the biggest Christmas in years, and Mr. Grayson had to break in the new stockroom clerk—"

"New stockroom clerk?" Chip interrupted.

Mitzi nodded. "That's right. Mr. Grayson will tell you about it."

"What about the fountain and food court?" Soapy asked.

"We just couldn't keep up with the extra business."

"With all the extra help he put on?" Soapy said in surprise.

"*New* help, Soapy. Don't forget that you and Fireball and Whitty were away, and most of the new people had never worked behind a fountain before. Oh, Soapy, would you please go upstairs to the office and ask Cara to come down and take my place?"

"Cara?"

Mitzi nodded at Soapy. "That's right. Cara Davis. She's the new cashier. Cara's a freshman. You'll like her, Soapy! Long blond hair and blue eyes, just like yours. Really cute!"

"You're kidding!"

"Go see. She's in Mr. Grayson's office."

Soapy hustled away, and, between customers, Mitzi told Chip she hadn't seen her employer since he had become ill. "Mrs. Grayson has been taking care of everything," she explained. "She comes down in the mornings to open up and then comes back again at night to help me close out the store. She's awfully worried."

An elderly lady placed some toothpaste, a greeting card, and a small plant on the counter, and Chip smiled and nodded at her before politely moving aside. Then he heard Soapy's "Ahem!" and turned to face the redhead and the new cashier.

"Ahem!" Soapy said again, rolling his eyes eloquently toward the girl beside him. "Chip, this is Cara Davis. Cara, this is Chip Hilton."

Mitzi's description of the new cashier had been too modest. Cara Davis was a knockout. Soapy was rolling his eyes and tripping over his own feet as Chip acknowledged the introduction. Chip started to say something to her, but the new cashier was too quick for him. She turned away and joined Mitzi behind the desk.

Mitzi swiftly tallied the sales slips and counted the contents of the cash register. "There you go, Cara," she said hastily. "Everything checks. It's all yours." She turned to Chip. "We can go now, Chip."

"What do you want me to do?" Soapy asked.

"Just wait," Mitzi said, smiling.

"Wait—" Soapy interrupted. He glanced at Cara and exclaimed, "You mean wait here, I hope."

"On the customers, Soapy," Mitzi said sweetly. "Just wait on the *customers*."

Soapy grinned. "Oh!" he said happily. "I get it! You want me to turn my dynamic personality loose and win back all the customers Grayson's lost while I was gone. Nothing to it! See you later."

Mr. and Mrs. George Grayson lived in a beautiful home on a golf course about ten miles from the business section of University. Despite the slippery streets, Mitzi made good time. She pulled her small car into the driveway and parked next to two pine trees decorated for the holidays in red bows. "Pretty, isn't it?" Mitzi commented as she and Chip climbed the brick front steps to the porch. Mrs. Grayson had evidently seen them pull in, because she opened the door just as Chip's finger was about to press the doorbell.

She welcomed them warmly and invited them in out of the biting cold. Chip helped Mitzi remove her coat and then Mrs. Grayson led them into the large den. Their employer was sitting in a wing chair in front of a fireplace still decorated with Christmas garlands.

Grayson turned in his chair as they entered and extended a hand to each of them. "Come here, you two, and sit down by the fire. Glad to see you, Chip. I hope I haven't spoiled your holiday."

Chip was shocked by his employer's pale, fragile appearance. Although the man was sitting, Chip quickly noted his weight loss. The friendly smile and warm greeting couldn't conceal the fact that George Grayson was seriously ill. It didn't seem possible that he could have changed so much in little more than a week. Chip forced a smile. "Not at all, Mr. Grayson," he said. "School starts tomorrow."

"I know. But you could have been home today."

Chip nodded. "That's right, but I would have been dead tired tomorrow."

"Like I am," George Grayson said. "Fine thing! I'm the only one who *isn't* on the job."

"You have been a little too much on the job," Mrs. Grayson said softly.

George Grayson's face stilled. "I guess that's right," he said, smiling ruefully. "Well, anyway, Chip, my doctor has ordered me to take a rest. I've got to go away for a couple of weeks to rest and sleep." He deliberated a second and then continued. "That's where you come in."

"I see," Chip said, nodding. But he didn't see. His mind was all jumbled up with a lot of thoughts, and they didn't add up to anything at all. Why send for him? What did Mr. Grayson mean when he said that was where he came in? What was this all about?

Then his employer's voice—sharp and clear—broke through his thoughts.

"Chip," Mr. Grayson said softly, "I'm putting you in complete charge of the store."

CHAPTER 3

College Stockroom Boy

"IN CHARGE of the store," Chip echoed weakly. He looked from Mitzi Savrill to Mrs. Grayson. Mitzi's eyes were shining with pride, and Mrs. Grayson was smiling and nodding her head. He shifted his glance to his employer. "Me?" he repeated. "In charge of the store?"

The ill man nodded. "That's right," he said quietly.

"But I'm not a pharmacist or a business person," Chip protested, shaking his head uncertainly. "And I've never had any experience at managing a store. Mr. Grayson, it's the biggest store in University!"

"I know," Grayson said thoughtfully.

"It's a big responsibility, sir."

"That's right!"

The muscles in Chip's chest tightened, and his breathing felt ragged, as if he had just completed the first half of a basketball game. The beating of his heart was like a bass drum. He hadn't expected anything like this. *In complete charge of the store! What about school? And what about basketball?* The cozy den was silent except for the sizzles and sharp crackles of the burning logs in the fireplace. Mrs. Grayson broke the silence and it was just as if she had read Chip's thoughts.

"Mr. Grayson doesn't expect you to miss school or basketball, Chip. He wants you to continue with your life just as you have in the past."

"Right!" Grayson said, nodding his head. "As far as experience is concerned, Chip, you've had a lot more than I had when I took over the store. Anyway, I believe in giving young people responsibilities. It keeps them out of trouble and helps them grow."

"Unfortunately," Mrs. Grayson interrupted, "neither Mr. Grayson nor I have any relatives who can step in to help with this emergency. As you know, our daughters are all grown and married and live out of state. There's just no way they can pitch in this time.

"No, we've given the decision a lot of thought, Chip, and Mr. Grayson—" She stopped and smiled toward Mitzi and then continued. "Mr. Grayson, Mitzi, and I all agree that you are the logical person to assume the responsibility."

"Absolutely!" Mr. Grayson said decisively. "I've hired another cashier, and Mitzi will work in my office. And to make it easier for you, I've put another full-time employee in the stockroom."

"Skip Miller and I can handle it, Mr. Grayson."

"Not if you're going to do all the things I've got in mind for you to do. By the way, I want you to help settle in Lonnie Freeman, the new man, right away." A spell of coughing racked his slender body, and he waited a moment before continuing.

"Now to get back to you. Besides supervising the supplies, inventories, and store stock, you will do all the ordering. When you get right down to it, you're the only one who knows the locations and methods we use to keep our supplies at replacement levels." He paused and studied Chip for a moment. "That's right, isn't it?"

Chip nodded. "I guess so, sir."

"Well, then it's settled. Mitzi will keep the records and make all the deposits, and you will be in charge of all personnel."

Grayson glanced briefly at Mitzi before continuing. "Steve Dixon and Sam Decker will cooperate fully, but you will no doubt find Kurt Welch a little grouchy. Don't pay any attention to his moods. He and I have been feuding for years. He's a confirmed grouch and an expert at needling if he thinks he can get under your skin. But he's harmless, and the reason I've kept him on all these years is that he's the best pharmacist I've ever known."

Chip made no response, but he visualized Kurt Welch. There was no doubt that the man was an efficient pharmacist, but he was arrogant and impatient with the other employees and exceedingly unpopular.

"Chip, I want you to spend as much time as you can at the store," Mr. Grayson continued. "Sam Decker can have your breakfast, lunch, and dinner sent up for you every day, and I would like you to eat in my office. I realize that opening up the store in the morning and closing up at night will be an additional chore, but it would help Mrs. Grayson and me a great deal."

"I can manage, Mr. Grayson."

"I suppose you wonder why I place so much confidence in you two young people," Mr. Grayson said, nodding at Chip and Mitzi. "Chip, I have always been impressed by your approach to the stockroom responsibilities. And to be perfectly frank with you, I have hoped for some time that you might develop an interest in the business. As far as Mitzi is concerned, she's practically grown up in the store."

George Grayson had written a list of points to be discussed on a piece of paper, and he methodically checked each one off and discussed it thoroughly before going on to the next item. Two hours later he concluded the meeting by presenting Chip with a set of keys. "There they are," he said, smiling weakly. "You have every key in the place. Dixon, Mitzi, and you have the only keys to the front door. I guess that's it. Mrs. Grayson will come down to the store a little later to tell everyone you are in charge. How about a little lunch now?"

Chip glanced at Mitzi, and when she shook her head, he joined her in declining the invitation. "I'm not a bit hungry," he said. "Soapy and I had a late breakfast at the student union. I think you ought to get some rest."

"I think so too," Mrs. Grayson said. "Perhaps we can talk in the living room for a moment before you go," she murmured to Chip and Mitzi.

Grayson nodded his consent and shook hands with them. Then he watched them until Mrs. Grayson softly closed the door to the den. "I'll just whip up some hot chocolate," she said. "Make yourselves at home in the living room." She nodded to a room just down the hall.

Chip and Mitzi admired the beautifully decorated seven-foot tall Christmas tree that dominated one corner of the large living room. Then Chip sank down on one of the chairs flanking both sides of another fireplace. "Why *me,* Mitzi? I'll never be able to do all of it."

"Chip, you *have* to do it," Mitzi said firmly. "There isn't anyone else."

Mrs. Grayson returned with a tray on which she had placed three red and green Christmas mugs filled with steaming hot chocolate dotted with miniature marshmallows. Chip smiled when he noticed they were the kind Soapy liked so much.

Mitzi and Chip chatted easily about their holidays and then, just as Chip and Mitzi were ready to leave, Mrs. Grayson took Chip's arm. "Chip, as you could see, Mr. Grayson is nearly exhausted. We appreciate your help more than we can say. And," she smiled now, "Mr. Grayson and I trust you as if you were our son."

A few minutes later, Mitzi and Chip were back in the car and retracing the route to Grayson's. Mitzi was quiet and thoughtful, and Chip's mind flooded with a thousand and one questions. How was he going to find enough time for classes, studying, basketball, *and* managing the store? It had been difficult enough before. Now, with the responsibility of opening and closing Grayson's, he would be busy every minute of the day. Where in the world would he find the time? And how about basketball trips?

There were no customers in front of the cashier's desk when they walked in. Cara Davis saw him, but there was little interest in her calm, cool glance. She was all business. Soapy was busy, too, but he gave Chip a big "Hello!" as if he hadn't seen him for a week.

"The new help seems nice enough," Soapy said significantly, lifting an eyebrow toward the cashier's desk.

Chip continued through the crowd and opened the stockroom door. Inside he found Skip Miller and the new clerk checking a shipment against an invoice. Skip glanced up quickly, and a smile of welcome crossed his face. "Hey! Chip!" he exclaimed. He grabbed Chip's hand and shook it vigorously. "Welcome home! Am I glad to see you! This is Lonnie Freeman. Lonnie, this is our boss, Chip Hilton."

Chip shook Lonnie's hand and smiled. "Mr. Grayson is the only boss around here. Glad to meet you, Lonnie. Welcome."

Freeman was looking first at Chip and then at Skip. "I never believed it until now," he said. "You guys could be identical twins."

"Skip's better looking," Chip said lightly.

"Oh, sure!" Skip said quickly. "Hey, Chip, you guys did all right in the tournament. How did it feel to break the Garden record?"

"Pretty good."

Skip turned to the new assistant. "Seventy-three points," he said, his voice filled with awe. "Seventy-three! That's as many points as our whole *team* makes in a game."

Lonnie Freeman nodded his head in admiration. "I couldn't make seventy-three points in a season."

"You could if you were playing with the guys on our team," Chip said. "They gave me the ball every time there was a shot."

"That Southwestern player must be quite a ballplayer," Skip observed. "What's his name?"

"Kinser. They call him 'Swish' Kinser."

"I read in *Sports Illustrated* that he's averaging over forty points a game. Hey, by the way, Chip, what kind of a guy is the new coach?"

"I don't know, Skip. I haven't met him yet."

"Well, I know a little from what I've been reading about him in the sports pages. Bill Bell said in his column in the *Herald* that Stone was going to use the Northern State possession game; he said you would lose your national scoring lead if he did."

"*My* scoring isn't important."

"You're the only person in this town who doesn't think it's important. I'll bet every basketball fan in the country knows your average."

"I know I do!" Lonnie added. "I knew it before I even dreamed of working at Grayson's or meeting you."

"But there's more to basketball than shooting," Chip said, smiling. "Anyway, right now I think we'd better forget about basketball and get to work."

"That's right," Skip agreed. "We've been swamped. I guess you know about Mr. Grayson."

"Yes, I saw him this morning. That's another reason to get busy. Have you guys had lunch yet?"

"We don't want any," Skip said, glancing at Freeman. "Right, Lonnie?"

Freeman nodded. "Right! We'll get something later."

Soapy came back to the stockroom with a tray of cheeseburgers and milk shakes at four o'clock. "This is the first break I've had," he said, glancing significantly toward Chip.

"Mitzi was right about the fountain. I'll sure be glad when Fireball and Whitty get back."

"They'll probably be back tonight," Skip said. "School starts tomorrow."

"And basketball too," Chip added.

"And," Soapy added, "we'll meet the new coach tomorrow. Well, back to my admiring fans! See you later."

Chip finished his burger and went back to work. A little later the stockroom phone rang. Skip answered it. He listened a moment, said, "Sure, thanks," and then hung up. "That was Mitzi, Chip. She said Mrs. Grayson wants you to come up to the office right away."

Chip drew in a deep breath. This was the moment he had been dreading all afternoon. He wasn't worried about the reactions of the younger employees, which covered the fountain bunch and the college extras who worked in the food court area and the pharmacy. But the older men like Kurt Welch and Steve Dixon and Sam Decker were a different story. They had been with Grayson's for a long time. How would they react?

In preparing for the moment, he visualized each man. Welch was short, rotund, slow-moving, and a bit of a shirker. He was bald, and heavy jowls of fat hung down from his cheeks. The man was short-tempered and grumpy. He had little patience with everyone—sometimes even the customers.

Steve Dixon was in charge of the left side of the store where all the over-the-counter medicines, cosmetics, and toiletry articles were located. His section adjoined the prescription department. Dixon was tall, slender, friendly, industrious, and, in Chip's opinion, just the type of man to manage a store. It was hard to understand why Mr. Grayson hadn't placed him in charge.

Sam Decker was in charge of the novelties, greeting cards, and film processing on the right side of the store, as well as the soda fountain and food court. Sam was middle-aged, on the short side, and quick in his movements. He was precise in his work, friendly, and cooperative. He, too, would have been a good choice for a manager. *Well, there isn't anything to do except face it,* he thought.

Chip had never counted the number of steps leading to the balcony where George Grayson's office was located. Now he wished there were a couple hundred more of them. He walked slowly up to the balcony landing, hesitated a second, and then knocked on the door of the office. Mrs. Grayson called for him to come in. He opened the door.

She was sitting behind her husband's large cherry desk, and sitting in chairs around the office were Mitzi, Kurt Welch, Steve Dixon, and Sam Decker. Mitzi smiled at him, and Dixon and Decker nodded. Kurt Welch gazed steadily at the opposite wall, apparently unaware of his presence.

"Sit down, Chip," Mrs. Grayson said, motioning to a chair beside the desk. "Chip," she continued, when he was seated, "I have just told Mr. Welch, Mr. Dixon, and Mr. Decker that you will be in full charge of the store during Mr. Grayson's absence. They understand that all employees will be responsible to you and also that you will work out of this office and from this desk. I have also asked them to inform the members of their departments of your appointment. I am sure you will receive full cooperation from everyone."

"Count on me, Chip," Steve Dixon said.

"Me too," Sam Decker added, smiling.

Mrs. Grayson hesitated and glanced at Kurt Welch, but he said nothing and stared stonily ahead. She smiled briefly and continued. "I want you to know that I greatly appreciate your understanding and cooperation. Chip, I'd like you and Mitzi to please stay behind for a few minutes. I want to speak with you."

The three department heads filed out of the room, with the surly pharmacist in the lead. Welch barely nodded to Mrs. Grayson, but Dixon and Decker both asked how she was holding up and assured her that everything would be all right. After they were gone, Mrs. Grayson gave Chip the keys to the desk and asked Mitzi to show him the combination to the office safe. She left a few minutes later, and Chip and Mitzi went back to work.

On his way to the stockroom Chip passed in front of the prescription counter. Kurt Welch was talking to one of his assistants. The angry pharmacist apparently didn't see him, but Chip noted that Welch raised his voice as he approached.

"That's right," Welch said sarcastically. "Your new boss is the college stockroom boy. I knew Grayson had lost a lot of weight. He must have lost his mind too."

A hot surge of anger raced through Chip's entire being, and his first impulse was to face up to Welch and have a showdown right then and there. But his better judgment prevailed, and he continued past the counter and on to the stockroom. *Stockroom boy!* he rasped angrily to himself. Welch and everyone else would find out whether George Grayson was out of his mind by putting him in charge of the store. He wasn't going to give up without trying.

CHAPTER 4

Hired to Win Games

THE LOCKER ROOM was buzzing with the usual confusion and chatter, but an air of expectancy hovered palpably above everything. Chip could tell by the voices and actions of his teammates and Andre Gilbert, the student manager, that they were all gripped by the same feeling. Everyone else was just as keyed up as he was in anticipation of the first meeting with the new coach, Mike Stone.

Chip glanced at Murph Kelly. The veteran trainer was tough, and a player never got very close to him, but Chip could tell that the older man was agitated. Murph had been a little more abrupt than usual in his conversation. Chip leaned back against his locker and relaxed. Most of the players were dressed, but a few, with Soapy among them, were still lacing their shoes or adjusting their practice uniforms.

"How about a ball, Murph?" Dom Di Santis asked.

"Nope," Kelly barked. "I told you before and I'm telling you again. No ball!"

"But we always shoot around before practice."

"Coach Stone said there was to be no more shooting around before practices."

"But why?" Di Santis persisted.

"No shooting before practices?" Jimmy Chung asked. "What's with that?"

Murph Kelly stopped taping ankles, straightened up, and glared first at Di Santis and then at Chung. "How would *I* know?" he demanded. "Why don't you ask him?"

"Well, that's a different approach," Rudy Slater drawled.

Kelly smiled grimly. "It sure is! Lots of things are going to be different around here."

"What do you mean?"

"You'll find out. Now all you guys who are dressed get out of here and get up in the bleachers. Dad Young said for me to have you ready for a meeting at 3:30 to meet the new coach, and I've got exactly five minutes to do it—

"Come on, Smith! How come you're *always* last? Slow as molasses, you are . . . same on the court too!"

Kelly glared around the room and then centered his attention on J. C. Tucker. "You're no better, Tucker," he growled. "Get with it!"

Chip waited until Soapy and Speed finished lacing their shoes. Then the three friends walked shoulder to shoulder out into the hall, up the players' aisle to the court, and into the bleachers. The players who were already there were unusually quiet, and Soapy elbowed Chip in the ribs and jerked his head toward the main entrance.

Dad Young and a tall man dressed in a warm-up suit were standing near the door. Chip studied the new coach. Stone was about six-five in height and weighed about 220 pounds. He had thick black hair.

Murph Kelly and the rest of the players arrived, so Kelly sent Andre Gilbert to tell Dad Young that everyone was present and waiting in the bleachers.

The two men approached slowly, and Chip had a closer view of Mike Stone. The man had intelligent, dark brown eyes, a swarthy complexion, long arms, and what Coach Rockwell would call "basketball hands." Chip then shifted his attention to Dad Young. The athletic director was also a big man. He was tall and heavily built and had been directing State's athletics for many years. Everybody liked Dad Young—players, coaches, students, alumni, and townspeople. *And,* Chip thought, *like most strong men, Dad Young possesses a gentle demeanor.*

Young paused in front of the little group and nodded to Kelly. "Thanks, Murph. Hello, men. First, I want to congratulate you on your fine showing in the tournament in Madison Square Garden. We're all proud of you. I wish Coach Corrigan were here so I could thank him in front of you for a job well done, but he's in England and is a college student again—albeit an older one." He paused and smiled. "It's hard to imagine Jim as a student. We're going to miss him in a lot of ways.

"Now to get to the purpose of this meeting. I wanted to make sure that our new coach got off on the right foot. First, I can tell you that the search committee screened more than one hundred applicants before deciding on Coach Stone.

"I'm sure that most of you have read about him in the papers and know that he played for Northern State for three years and earned all-American honors. And since his graduation, he's been coaching at his alma mater.

"We don't expect him to install his system overnight, and we don't expect miracles when it comes to winning. Naturally, however, we want to go as far as we can. I've told the coach he can count on your cooperation.

"Coach Stone impressed the committee as being the type of man needed to lead State to the front in the national picture. We do well in our conference, but we never seem to have what it takes to go all the way. The university feels our new coach can put us in the national picture and keep us there.

"The less time I take with this introduction, the more time you players will have to work. Men, I am happy to present your new State University basketball coach, Mike Stone."

Chip joined his teammates in the applause, which lasted until Dad Young raised a hand. Facing Stone, Young said, "Young man, since you watched Northern State beat us in New York a few days ago, I'm sure you know most of our players. However, I'm going to ask each of them to step forward and introduce himself. Since you're the captain, Hilton, suppose you start it off."

Chip took a long stride down from his seat in the bleachers and extended his hand. Chip possessed a strong grip, but he was far from prepared for the viselike clasp the new coach clamped on his hand. "Glad to meet you, Hilton," Stone said. "It's a real pleasure."

One by one, the players shook hands with Stone and then returned to their seats. Dad Young shook Stone's hand, wished him luck, and turned away.

Mike Stone waited until Dad Young had left the court and then asked Murph Kelly for a ball. "I feel a lot more comfortable with a ball in my hands," he said, smiling briefly.

"Men," he continued, "I saw you play in New York, and I am aware that you are a good run-and-shoot team. But I believe you will be far stronger with a possession attack. Besides, it's the approach to basketball that I know best.

"Don't misunderstand me. I think Coach Corrigan's offense is a good one. However, I learned to play the Northern State way, and the control game is my game. So we'll start working on it right away.

"First, however, I want you to understand how I feel about basketball. Basketball is a cold proposition. It's just like big business, a dog-eat-dog world. I ought to know," he said grimly. Looking down at the ball, he twirled it on his fingertips several times. "My approach to coaching," he continued slowly, "is just like the approach of a corporate executive to a business proposition.

"First in importance is organization. I plan and outline my season, my practice sessions, and the duties of the coaches, managers, and trainers. I photocopy everything they are expected to do in detail. This means nothing is left to chance, and most misunderstandings are eliminated.

"I also chart player and team performances. The information recorded on the charts provides an accurate breakdown of the performance of each player in each scrimmage, practice, and game. The records cover rebounds, interceptions, time played, scoring attempts, shots made, shooting percentage, fumbles, violations, and anything and everything concerned with basketball.

"My student managers place and summarize the information on the charts so the record is available when needed. You will find this information and many other basketball items posted on the basketball bulletin boards.

"Bulletin boards play a big role in my coaching. You will be expected to consult them each day and know what they contain. I use the boards for all notices concerning practices, trips, schedules, and other important basketball information.

"The white board and the strategy board are important teaching methods. I'll use them in strategy sessions and during practices to present plays and to clear up player questions. Now all this use of paper, strategy boards, and white boards may seem unnecessary to you, but in my opinion, it's all vital to winning. And after all, that's what I've been hired to do: win games!

"I have photocopied the basic circulation and plays of our control game, and you'll be given these at the end of practice. Right now, I want to use the white board to outline the possession offense that we'll use."

Kelly and Gilbert had rolled the gleaming white board out in front of the bleachers, and Stone quickly sketched a formation.

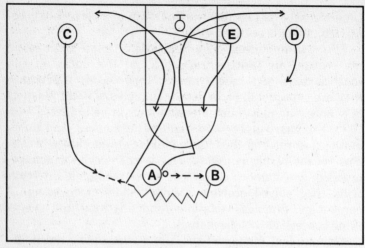

"When I played ball, there was no shot clock in college basketball. But now we'll use up all the time we can, before we take a shot. I'm sure all of you are familiar with this figure eight give-and-go weave. However, I want to take time to discuss its importance in our system. Players A, B, C, and D are using the weave, passing the ball and cutting through the lane toward the basket, and then fanning out to the corners and up the sidelines. All sorts of plays develop from this circulation, and I use its continuity pattern in setting up my control offense.

"Player E is the big man. He operates in the pivot position near the basket and out to a post position around the free-throw circle. Are there any questions?" Stone waited a moment and then gestured for Andre to erase the board.

Chip knew the four-man give-and-go weave and plays by heart, but he gave Mike Stone close attention. Jim Sullivan, one of State's football coaches, had scouted for Coach Corrigan and had gone over Northern State's offense and defense a number of times. Chip listened carefully, but at the same time he couldn't help comparing Mike Stone with his former coach, Jim Corrigan.

The new coach was grim, determined, and dedicated, and he was probably a better technical coach than Jim Corrigan. But Chip wasn't sure Stone's basketball philosophy would sit well with the State players.

Basketball might be big business to Stone, but to Jim Corrigan and the guys on the team, as Chip knew them, it was a sport—a challenge coupled with team play and fun. Jim Corrigan had combined serious work at his job with friendly consideration for his players. With Corrigan, the players' welfare came first and winning games came second.

Stone had finished the diagram now, and Chip concentrated on the board. "This will give you an idea of the play of the center," Stone explained, pointing to the circled E. "The center, E, waits until a player cutting toward the basket screens behind his opponent, X. Then he cuts around the screen to the other side of the lane. Naturally, the ball is passed to him if he breaks free. This cutting back and forth follows each screen."

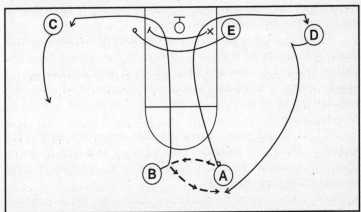

He gestured toward the board. "Any questions?"

Not one hand raised, and Andre Gilbert again erased the board. Stone quickly drew another diagram. "This is the freeze. Study it for a moment."

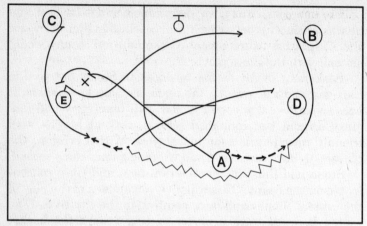

Stone waited for them to concentrate and then continued. "The center of the court is kept open so the opponents have trouble getting a double-team situation. Player A passes the ball to B cutting up the right sideline behind D. Then A cuts *away* from the ball and sets a screen behind teammate E's guard on the left side of the court.

"Player E cuts around A's screen, toward the basket and then on to the right corner. If he breaks free, B will pass the ball to him. If E does not break free, B will dribble across court—using a left-hand dribble, of course—and pass the ball to C, who is cutting out from the left corner behind A, who replaced E.

"Player B will then cut away and set a screen for D's guard on the right sideline. This passing and cutting away from the receiver continues until a play is possible or time runs out. Any questions?"

Again there were no questions. Stone waited a moment and then sent them out on the court. "Start with your warm-up drill and put some zip into it!" he said sharply. "We'll make up for the break right now."

The practice was a revelation, almost a shock. Stone's coaching methods were totally different from those they had come to know with Jim Corrigan. Stone drove them without a break for two hours.

Chip and his teammates didn't mind work; they always hustled during practices, and they subscribed wholeheartedly to Coach Corrigan's philosophy that a team played the same way it practiced. But the Statesmen weren't used to a coach who drove them fiercely and relentlessly with shouts and yells and, not infrequently, with obvious impatience. Several times during the practice he expressed disgust and irritation when one of them made a mistake.

"Aw, c'mon! Didn't anyone *ever* teach you how to pivot?"

"This is ridiculous! Here! Let me show you!"

"A rookie high school player could do better than that!"

It was a new experience for the Statesmen; they were confused, and their confusion was reflected in their play. Much of their confidence disappeared, which only led to more mistakes and misplays. Chip noticed his teammates' grim side glances when Stone become overly impatient. As always, Soapy was hustling for all he was worth, but he cast foreboding glances toward Chip and Speed during several of Stone's outbursts.

It was nearly 6:30 when Stone ordered the players to the bleachers and told Gilbert to distribute the photocopies. "That wasn't bad for a start," he said briskly, "but a lot of you guys sure got out of shape during vacation. I'm disappointed. I *know* Coach Corrigan told you to keep in condition. But now I'm going to outline *my* training rules."

Speaking slowly and firmly, Stone accentuated each word. "First," he said, "the gym will be open at three o'clock and you will not—and I repeat, *you will not*—be permitted on the floor before that time. I always supervise prepractice shooting, and you'll find me here when you report.

"And get this straight and clear. You are expected to be prompt and on time every day unless your schedule calls for a late class. In that case, you will be allowed thirty minutes after your class ends to get to the gym and out on the floor.

"Second, all practices must be attended. No excuses and no exceptions!

"Third, everyone must be off the streets and in their rooms by 10:30. And I mean *every night* except Saturdays. That's all! Good night."

CHAPTER 5

Exception for the Star

MIKE STONE pivoted and was halfway across the court before the Statesmen had a chance to move. Chip was the first to get to his feet and start for the locker room. Soapy was practically stepping on his heels. Behind him, Chip could hear his teammates muttering, but he was too busy with his own thoughts to pay attention to their comments.

"It can't be done!" Soapy said. "Lots of nights we don't get through work until 10:30."

Chip nodded. "I know, Soapy."

"What do we do?"

"Talk to him. Get late curfew permission. That's all we *can* do."

"What if he says no?"

"Then I'm out of basketball."

"You mean you'll quit?"

"That's right. I can't do anything else without letting Mr. Grayson down. And I won't do that."

"What about me?"

"You have no problem. Fireball or Whitty can take your late shift."

Soapy stopped so quickly his shoes squeaked on the hardwood floor. "Nothing doing! If you quit basketball, *I* quit basketball."

"All right, have it your way, but let's not stand here. We're late for work."

They were the first to reach the locker room and the first to change back into their jeans and sweaters.

Chip was deep in thought. Stone's curfew rule had created real problems for his responsibilities at Grayson's. Still, he couldn't help hearing the remarks of his teammates.

Dom Di Santis banged the door of his locker with his fist and scowled when Murph Kelly glowered at him. "Things are different, all right, Murph," he said significantly.

"You can say that again," J. C. Tucker agreed. "We're in business!"

"Basketball may be *his* whole life," Speed Morris observed pointedly, "but it's far from being *mine.*"

The Statesmen were still discussing the workout when Chip and Soapy said, "'Night, guys, Murph," and set out across the parking lot. A new snowfall had coated the slippery spots on the open lot during practice, and the going was slow and dangerous. To add to their discomfort, a driving northwest wind cut sharply against their faces, making conversation difficult.

"Coach Corrigan gave us a late curfew," Soapy managed in a muffled voice. "You think Stone will give us a break?"

Chip nodded. "I think so. Stop worrying."

About ten minutes later, they were stamping the snow off their shoes in front of Grayson's. The parking lot across the street from the store's main entrance was packed with cars, and they watched as a shopper barely edged his car into the last spot. The store was crowded with shoppers, and students lined the fountain and filled every booth. "Doesn't *any-*

body eat at the student union?" Soapy sputtered. "And on a night like this!"

Chip shook his head and grinned to himself. Soapy was always pretending to dislike his work, but Chip knew the redhead would have been bored to death if he had nothing to do. He also noticed that his friend cheered up enough to smile and wink at Cara Davis as they passed the cashier's desk. Chip led the way on through the store and pushed open the door to the stockroom.

Skip Miller was perched precariously on a ladder and nearly fell off in his haste to get down when he saw Chip and Soapy. "What kind of a guy is he?" he demanded.

"A big biz entrepreneur!" Soapy said sarcastically, reaching for his fountain uniform.

"What do you mean?"

Soapy snorted as he pulled on his red and blue polo shirt with the stenciling "Grayson's" on the back and "Soapy Smith" above the front pocket. "Humph! Ask Chip! I've got something more important to think about. See you later."

Skip turned to Chip. "What's wrong with him?"

"You know Soapy," Chip smiled.

Skip grinned. "Well, at least enough to know he isn't too crazy about Mike Stone. What happened?"

"Nothing, Skip."

Skip eyed Chip narrowly and nodded. "Of course not! I should have known you wouldn't say anything." He studied Chip a moment and then continued. "Soapy liked Coach Corrigan a lot, didn't he?"

"Very much, Skip. We all did. How did *your* practice go?"

"Great!" Skip said quickly. Then he brought the conversation back to his starting point. "Mike Stone is tough, isn't he?" He paused and then added questioningly, "Real tough?"

Chip shook his head. "No, but he is a driver."

"I heard he was only an assistant coach before he got the State job. Maybe it was too big a step for him."

"I don't think so, Skip. Have you eaten yet?"

"Not yet, but Lonnie will be back soon. I can wait."

"No, you go on home. Take the evening off and do some studying."

"I haven't got any homework—"

"You can do some reading then."

Skip smiled. "You sound like my father. Thanks, I'll take you up on it. See you tomorrow, Chip."

Chip busied himself in the stockroom at his computer until Freeman returned. Then, between calls from the various departments for supplies or replacements, he outlined the new clerk's responsibilities and questioned him about the general operation. Chip smiled to himself. Skip Miller was a fine teacher. Lonnie Freeman already possessed a keen knowledge of his duties.

The method of handling the prescription medicines had to be changed because of Mr. Grayson's absence, and Chip explained the new procedure. "Each night before closing, the stock is to be checked in with Mitzi Savrill or me. Then we'll put everything in the safe for the night. Mitzi or I will issue them again the next morning."

It was 10:30 before Chip felt sure the new clerk was completely familiar with all the details of the stockroom operation. Then he sent Freeman to collect the medications and hurried to help Mitzi balance the registers. Soapy joined Fireball Finley and Philip "Whitty" Whittemore after the fountain closed, and the three workers headed for their favorite eating spot, Pete's Restaurant. The little eating place was located on Tenth Street, just a few steps from Grayson's.

"We'll wait for you at Pete's," Soapy promised.

Mitzi had completed her cash check by the time Freeman got to the office with the valuables box, and they placed everything in the safe, locked it, and dimmed the light. Chip made a final check at the side and back doors and then locked the main entrance. Mitzi offered Chip a lift home, but he declined and headed for the restaurant, shivering at the impact of the biting wind.

Pete's Restaurant was a popular meeting place for members of State's athletic teams, but Chip liked the place because Jimmy Chung, State's little dribbling wizard, worked there as a counterman. Then, too, the owner of the restaurant, Pete Thorpe, was a personal friend.

Thorpe was pouring coffee for a lone customer at the counter when Chip entered. "Hiya, Chipper," he called. He jerked his head toward a booth in the corner. "If you're looking for the politician, he's over there."

Soapy stood up and glared at Thorpe. "I always spoke well of you," he said accusingly. "This brings an end to a beautiful friendship. If I'm elected, I'll close the place. What'll you have, Chip?"

"Not a thing, Soapy. Come on! We're breaking training rules."

"I'll say you are," Thorpe interrupted. "I sent Jimmy home at ten o'clock."

"What's the difference whether it's an hour or an hour and a half?" Soapy said tiredly.

"A lot of difference when you're working!" Chip retorted swiftly.

"You guys are in big trouble either way," Thorpe said. "At least that's the impression I got from talking to Jimmy. The new coach seems to be quite a guy."

"Anyway," Chip said firmly, hoping to stop the discussion, "I'm going."

Soapy immediately capitulated. "All right, all right," he said quietly. "See you tomorrow, Pete. Good night, Fireball, Whitty."

When they reached the room they shared in Jefferson Hall, Soapy went right to bed. But Chip pulled on some sweats and sat down at his desk.

Soapy sat up and glared in protest. "I thought you were in a hurry to get to bed."

"Not to get to bed. To get home and do some studying. I'm falling behind in my work. Is the light bothering you?"

"Of course not. But don't work yourself to death."

"I'm not."

Soapy muttered something, threw himself back on his pillow, and pulled the covers up over his head. Chip studied until he couldn't keep his eyes open and then snapped out the desk light and crawled under his quilt.

It was tough to wake up when the alarm rang the next morning, but Chip forced his tired muscles into action and got on his feet. Soapy had an early class and, as was his custom, had set the alarm and slipped out of the room without a sound. Chip grinned in appreciation. The redhead was like that.

Thursday was one of Chip's short school days. After his last class he went to the store and worked straight through lunch. Later, when he could restrain his impatience no longer, he set out for Assembly Hall to see Coach Stone. He was the first player to show up, only to be told by Murph Kelly that Coach Stone usually arrived around two o'clock. While he waited impatiently, Chip read the notices and the player performance statistics on the bulletin board.

"How come you're so early?" someone said behind him. Chip turned quickly to see Mike Stone.

"I wanted to talk to you, Coach. I'd like to get late curfew permission."

"Late curfew?"

"Yes, sir. It's impossible for me to get home by 10:30."

"Impossible?"

"That's right. You see, Coach, I work at Grayson's every night."

"Every night?"

"Yes, sir. Six nights a week."

"Are you trying to tell me you would let a job interfere with your basketball? With team training?"

"Not with training, only with the curfew. I don't get to the dorm after work until around eleven o'clock. Last night it was 11:30."

"Eleven-thirty!"

"That's right."

Stone studied Chip for a long time and then shook his head uncertainly. "I don't get it. Your athletic scholarship certainly covers your expenses." The blood rushed to his face in a sudden burst of rage, and his angry voice rang through the empty hall. "What you're really trying to say is that you want me to make an exception in your case. Right? You want me to make an exception for the star! For Chip Hilton!

"Well, *Captain,* nothing doing!"

My Way or the Highway

STINGING ANGER flooded Chip for a breathtaking second, but he quickly reined himself in. With an act of will, he forced back the desire to lash out in anger. Regaining his composure, Chip backed away from Stone's angry, red face.

"I don't want you to make any exceptions for me, Coach," Chip said smoothly. "But I think you ought to know that I'm not at State on an athletic scholarship. I'm working my way through school."

"*Working* your way?"

"Yes, sir."

Stone had regained a measure of self-control, but he was still gripped by anger. "Are you trying to tell me you can't get an athletic scholarship?"

"No, sir, that's not it. It's just that I prefer to *work* my way through school. I want to play sports without any strings, just for the sake of the sport."

"A scholarship wouldn't make you dislike the game, would it?"

"No, sir, but I want to play basketball for fun. Getting a scholarship for playing is like getting paid."

"You're the only athlete *I* ever ran into with that philosophy."

"Soapy Smith feels the same way."

"He doesn't want a scholarship either?"

"No, sir."

"What about Corrigan?" Stone demanded. "He gave you late curfew permission?"

Chip nodded. "Yes, sir, and Soapy too."

"Where does Smith work?"

"Grayson's."

"How about football and baseball? You mean to tell me you had curfew exceptions in those sports too?"

"Yes, sir. We had the same privilege in both sports."

Stone seemed at a loss for words. He drew the frown lines between his eyebrows close together and eyed Chip steadily. His dark eyes were hard and uncompromising as they drilled into Chip's steady gaze. At last he drew a long breath and began to speak. "It's hard to believe. Frankly, I never heard of such a thing in Division I collegiate sports. I don't get it. Just what is this sports philosophy of yours?"

Chip had never tried to assemble his sports philosophy into a logical sequence, and he tried to figure out where to start. It wasn't easy. His attitude toward sports participation was all tied up with desires for physical action, a sense of belonging to a group, competition, team play, and the urge to win. His mind was working frantically but getting nowhere, so he decided to forget about trying to make a formal presentation.

"First," he began, "I like all games. I guess the reason for that is competition. When I play or try to play a game, I like to play well—at least, as well as or maybe a little better than the other guys in my group."

"You do that just fine," Stone said dryly.

The interruption broke Chip's thinking for a moment, but he plunged on without trying to organize his words. "I believe that to excel in something, anything, a person has to pay a price. In my case, I feel that the giving up of something enjoyable, such as personal freedom, loafing around with my friends, going to a show, or forcing myself to train when I would rather take it easy, is a sacrifice. Then, too, I like to work with a bunch of guys in a common cause and try to do something as part of a team."

Stone nodded his head in agreement. "Fine!" he said. "But you're no different in that respect than any of the players on scholarship. *They* practice and train when it would be more fun to go the movies or watch TV or loaf around."

"That part of it is all right," Chip agreed, "but the players on scholarships are getting paid to play, just as I get paid to work at Grayson's."

"But it's not money, right?"

"No, but tuition, fees, books, meals, and housing all represent money. There's a big difference between doing something for pay and doing it for fun."

"Don't you enjoy your work at Grayson's?"

Chip nodded. "Yes, I do."

"According to your way of thinking, then," Stone reasoned, "a player on scholarship doesn't enjoy playing. Do you think that's true of Di Santis, Slater, or Phillips?"

"No, sir, I don't. But I do think they are getting something that is measured in terms of money rather than the enjoyment that comes from playing for fun. Making sacrifices because a player loves a sport is a lot like patriotism. At least, that's the way I feel about it."

"You don't mean that players on scholarship aren't loyal to their school, do you?"

"No, not at all. Just about all colleges give athletic scholarships, but in my opinion they are wrong for *me* because they are compensating players to represent them. In the long run, any school that had the money and wanted to spend it that way could go all over the country and hire three or four outstanding players for every position on a team and win every game. But the players wouldn't be true representatives of the normal student body.

"And there's another side to it. Lots of guys and girls go to college without athletic scholarships, and they like to play on college teams. But the players on athletic scholarships are handpicked specialists, and the average student doesn't have a chance. The nonscholarship players would like to train and practice and strive for excellence the same as the handpicked players. Then, too, many of the scholarship players are imported from far away—"

"So? What's wrong with that?" Stone asked. "Many colleges and universities think it's important to attract students from other parts of the country and even other parts of the world just to spread ideas and cultures."

Chip nodded in agreement. "Right, but the imported athlete doesn't come to a college to spread ideas or cultures. He comes to represent the school in a sport, and he comes because he's paid to come—just as if he was a hired teacher. The better the player, the higher the compensation.

"I don't remember who it was, but a famous coach once said that in our own neighborhoods, and right around the corner, there are athletes who could be just as good as the stars from different states. He said that great players and teams would emerge from *any* given neighborhood if the young people from that area were given the opportunity to play and if some teacher or coach would sacrifice the time and patience to go out and work with them."

Stone stifled a laugh. "You sound almost like a social worker."

"I guess I do," Chip agreed and smiled for the first time. "Anyway, that's the way I feel."

Stone shrugged his shoulders and looked at his watch. "It's too much for me, Hilton. I'll have to give it a little more thought before making a decision. Right now we'd better get ready for practice."

Stone walked swiftly away as Chip went back to the locker room and sat down on the bench in front of his locker. He was still unnerved by the experience and wanted to relax.

Murph Kelly was tearing tape and sticking the long strips on the edge of one of the trainers' tables. He looked up and eyed Chip sympathetically. "Couldn't help overhearing, Chip," he said. "I wouldn't worry too much about it. He'll give you late curfew."

Before Chip could reply, Dom Di Santis, Jimmy Chung, Speed Morris, and Soapy arrived. They broke off their conversation as soon as they entered the locker room. Soapy and Speed saw Chip and walked swiftly over, dropping down beside him.

"What happened?" Soapy asked, his brows wrinkled in concern. "What did he say?"

Chip told them about Stone's reaction and what he had said. "He didn't make a decision. He said he would think it over."

"You mentioned me, didn't you?" Soapy asked.

"Of course." Chip smiled grimly.

"How about practice?" Speed asked. "You going to work out?"

"Sure! He said to get ready."

Soapy expanded like a balloon, and a confident grin spread across his lips. "Naturally," he said, swaggering to his feet. "How could Stone, ahem, the team, get along without *me?*"

That did it. Speed opened up on Soapy, and insults flew right and left as they went into one of their verbal sparring acts. Most of the players had arrived by now, and for the first time since their return from the holidays, the familiar good-natured spirit filled the State locker room.

Chip knew his teammates had an inkling of the curfew incident. He had noted their quick glances toward him when they entered the locker room and the measure of relief flooding their tense expressions when they saw him dressing. And when Murph Kelly said, "Let's go!" the Statesmen went out on the court with their spirits once again on a high level.

As captain of the team, Chip got a big lift out of his teammates' enthusiasm. They were alerted now; they were ready for Stone, for his coaching methods, and for his driving spirit. The Statesmen had a lot of pride mixed in with their love for basketball. They could take it as well as dish it out.

The locker room spirit carried over into the warm-up drill. The Brandon game was two days away, and the players wanted to be ready. Once again the shouts and yells and jibes and challenges rang out.

"Everybody hits!"

"Atta boy, Jimmy!"

"That's the way, guys!"

"Everybody does it!"

"Twenty in a row!"

"Twenty-one, twenty-two, twenty-three—"

"Gimme that rock!"

"Hey! Hey! Hey!"

Stone shouted and drove them, and the Statesmen shouted right along with him during the drills for the sheer love of action. But when it came to working on Stone's possession offense, the enthusiasm drained out of them—out of all of them. The team liked the running game. They liked the freedom and the sheer pleasure of cutting loose and running opponents off the boards, out of the gym, and out of the game. To them, holding the ball and passing and passing and passing and passing again were for the birds.

When Stone called it quits for the day, there was a glint of satisfaction in his eyes, but it wasn't heard in the harsh tone of his voice. "All right," he barked, "that's it. Everybody be on time tomorrow."

The last part of the workout had slowed down the enthusiasm of the players, but they were in better spirits than they had been the previous day. There was a bit of grumbling about the possession offense, but no signs of bitterness remained. Chip and Soapy dressed quickly and trudged through the snow to Grayson's.

Chip had outlined a regular routine in handling his responsibilities, but he was beginning to worry about his studies. The stockroom job had given him considerable time to study. The added responsibilities of George Grayson's office left little time for anything except work. That meant studying after he got home at night.

Everything was running smoothly at the store. Dixon and Decker were friendly and cooperative, and although Welch ignored him, the pharmacist kept himself busy in the pre-scription department. Everything was running smoothly.

Friday afternoon, Mrs. Grayson visited the store and talked briefly to Chip. "Mr. Grayson got away this morning for some rest," she said. "We're both very happy with the way things are going. Be sure to call me if there's anything you think I should know."

"Everything is fine, Mrs. Grayson," Chip assured her.

"How about basketball?"

"It's all right so far."

"What about your schoolwork?" she asked with concern. Before Chip could answer, she continued quickly, "Mr. Grayson wouldn't want you to get so involved with the store that you neglect your studies."

"I'll find time to study," Chip said confidently.

But Chip was worried about his grades, and as soon as Mrs. Grayson departed, he hit the books for an hour. Then he went to practice. It was a spirited workout. The Statesmen were raring to go in anticipation of the Saturday game, and the new coach found little need to employ his driving tactics.

When Stone ended the practice, he asked Chip to remain behind. He waited until the rest of the players had left the floor and then sat down in the first row of bleachers and motioned for Chip to sit beside him.

"I've been giving this curfew business a lot of thought, Hilton. Frankly, I can't see giving anyone special privileges. What's wrong with an athletic scholarship?"

"I explained that to you the other day, Coach."

"But it would take care of all your problems."

"But I don't want a scholarship, Coach. Neither does Soapy. We want to work our way. Besides, I couldn't leave Mr. Grayson in the lurch."

"In the lurch? Your job can't be *that* important."

"It wasn't as important until he got sick. He had to go away for a rest and he put me in charge of the store. I have to open up in the morning and close up at night. That's why I need a later curfew."

"You're in charge of the store? That's ridiculous! How can you go to school, study, play basketball, and manage a store all at the same time?"

"There isn't anyone else."

"You mean he doesn't have a relative or some full-time employee he can trust? Brother!" Stone said in disgust. "I start out on a new job with a set of training rules and you break them the very first night. Then it turns out you want to make it a regular practice."

"There isn't anything else I can do unless you want me to quit."

"That's silly! You know I can't let you quit. You're too valuable to the team. Besides, you're a national figure. Every State University official would be on my case—you know that!"

"It wouldn't be your fault."

"*Who* would believe that? No, Hilton, you can't quit and I can't let you quit. I can't do anything but give in. All right!" he grumbled bitterly. "Have it your way. There's no way I'm going to follow you around with a watch. You can have your late curfew, but that applies to you and *you* only. Smith isn't in charge of the store, too, is he?"

"No, sir."

"All right! Smith abides by the rules, and you go straight home after you close the store. Agreed?"

Chip nodded. "You can count on it, Coach."

"All right. See you tomorrow night."

CHAPTER 7

Walkathon
Basketball

ASSEMBLY HALL was jammed. A new coach, the seven-foot center, and a team that had come from nowhere to end up in third place in the Holiday Invitational Tournament in famed Madison Square Garden in New York—in addition to seeing the national scoring leader—all added up to a stellar attraction. That it was a conference opponent didn't hurt either. State University's students and fans were primed for a night of action.

The referee tossed the ball high in the air for the opening tap of the game, and Branch Phillips leaped upward with every bit of his seven feet of raw strength and power to snare the tap. Dom Di Santis came in high and fast, pulled in the ball, and whipped it to Slater in a high-post position on the right side of the court.

Chip cut around the post at full speed, and Rudy slipped the ball to him with a perfect handoff. Without breaking stride, he dribbled once and carried the ball up even with the rim and laid it against the board with perfect fingertip control to score the first two points of the game.

It was a beautiful play. The crowd roared in appreciation as the cheerleaders in red, white, and blue started the State University "Go SU! Go SU Go! Go! Go! SU!" chant.

Brandon University advanced slowly to their front court and set up a triple-post formation. Then they passed and screened and passed and screened until they could establish a double set-screen on the right side of the free-throw lane. The sideline pivot player faked a shot and then passed the ball to a backcourt teammate who drove around the double screen and went up for a jumper. His shot tied up the score.

State came down fast, and Chip and Rudy Slater teamed up on a turnaround play. Slater's guard failed to switch, and Chip was wide open under the basket. Slater hit him with a two-hand overhead pass, and the result was another easy two-pointer.

Once more Brandon advanced slowly to the front court. Then they started their deliberate roll attack. The fans didn't like it and began to count the passes. "Six, seven, eight, nine, ten, eleven—"

On the twelfth pass, a Brandon player attempted a shot. Phillips went high up on the board, made the rebound, and, twisting in the air, fired the ball to Chung, who was speeding far up the sideline. Jimmy, Slater, and Chip capitalized on the resulting three-on-two situation to score, and the crowd went wild!

The Statesmen scored several baskets in succession while holding Brandon scoreless. The score was 14-2 when Stone called for a time-out. Chip and his teammates trotted over to the bench and surrounded Stone, full of pep and confidence. Then they got a shock.

"What are you trying to do?" Stone demanded, the cords of his neck vibrating against his skin. "Wasn't it understood that we would set up our formation and work on the new offense?"

He glared around the circle of faces, sparing no one. "Well," he said, his face white and tense, "wasn't it?"

No one answered.

"Good players and good teams follow orders," Stone continued. "We'll settle *that* right now! You'll play my way or else. It's my way or the highway! *Sit down!* All but *you,* Phillips."

The irate coach turned to face the players who were standing behind him. "Tucker!" he called. "Report for Di Santis! Morris for Hilton! Reardon, go in for Chung! Hicks, sub for Slater! All right! Get out on that court and use the offense we've been practicing. Now, we'll play *my* way!"

Riding the bench was a new experience for Chip. He had sat out a few minutes from weariness and even missed a full game, but it had always been because of a rest or an injury. This was the first time he had ever been taken out of a game for failing to follow a coach's orders.

It was more of a misunderstanding than actual disobedience, he reflected. It had been so easy to score with the fast break that he hadn't given Stone's set formation a thought. He guessed his teammates had made the same mistake. He felt badly about the situation, but he forgot all about it as he watched the kind of basketball being played on the court. He followed the action closely, wincing inwardly from the bench as the game developed into a cagey cat-and-mouse contest.

Brandon would advance slowly into the offensive court and pass the ball ten or fifteen times until an open shot was possible. Then, as soon as they got the ball, the Statesmen would pursue the same tactics.

The fans didn't like it. Again, they began to count the passes, chanting in unison. Now they were counting for both teams. The Statesmen were playing Brandon's game now, and gradually, point by point, the visitors narrowed the margin. Just before the end of the half, Brandon passed State to lead 33-32 at the buzzer.

On the way to the locker room, many of the fans expressed their displeasure. "What are you trying to do, Coach, stall the ball the whole game?"

"Let 'em run! State's a run-and-shoot team."

"I thought basketball was a game of speed!"

Stone did not disrupt the regular locker room procedure, but when it was time to talk, he tore angrily into the players, directing his attack toward each member of the starting five. "You're the captain, Hilton," he said pointedly. "And you're supposed to set the example. You're supposed to control the ball club. And that's exactly what you *haven't* been doing.

"Chung! I know you can dribble, but basketball is a passing game. You're working in the backcourt with Hilton, and you're just as responsible for setting up the offense as he is! Cut out the dribbling and start passing!

"Phillips, you and I are in the same boat. Neither one of us has touched the ball yet in the front court. I'm not supposed to, but you're expected to score at least a *couple* of points and do *some* passing.

"Di Santis, Slater, you two stood around like you were glued to the floor. You're supposed to join up with Hilton and Chung in the screening and moving the ball, and I want to see you do it! Understand?"

Stone's face was set in hard lines, and his sharp eyes were glittering angrily. "Discipline is the most important thing in sports," he said, pausing to glare along the row of faces. "And," he continued, "a possession offense requires a lot of it. I can't and won't believe you haven't mastered the weave, and I expect you to go out there and prove it!"

He punched his right hand into the palm of his left. "Another thing! Forget the fans. They're as fickle as the weather. They brag about you when you win and whine about you when you lose. All we have to do is win and pretty soon they'll stop all the complaining and start supporting us.

"All right! Let's go back to the lineup the way you started. And this time I want to see you use *my* offense."

State's starting five tried hard to please Stone. On the possession arrow, Jimmy inbounded and Chip got it. Advancing slowly, he and Chung passed the ball back and forth until

Phillips, Di Santis, and Slater had taken their positions in Stone's possession formation. Then Chip started the weave. He and his teammates passed, screened, and cut and passed, screened, and cut. And they did it again and again.

When the passing and screening and cutting failed to provide a play and they had to start all over again, Chip could feel the tension and uncertainty building in his teammates. This wasn't basketball; it was a game of nerves. A game in which they passed and watched and passed and watched until they caught an opponent out of position or making a mistake—or until just seconds remained on the shot clock. Only then did a player cut for the basket and hope to receive a fast pass for a shot.

The fans hadn't expected this from State's starting five and once again began to count the passes. "Six, seven, eight, nine . . . ." The Statesmen were playing Brandon's game but managed to keep within striking distance only because they were better players, both as passers and shooters. But they didn't catch up. Every time they scored, Brandon matched the tally.

With seven minutes left to play, they were down by six points, and at the rate they were going, it was certain State University was doomed to defeat. Then, almost as if they had taken a time-out and decided to change their tactics, the Statesmen slipped back into their regular game and pressed for two quick baskets.

The additional points put them within striking distance of the visitors, and with the end of the game in sight and the home team fighting for their very lives, the fans rose to their feet en masse and began to urge the Statesmen on with frenzied cheers and yells.

A Brandon player scored with a long jumper to put the visitors four points ahead. Then, with Phillips and Di Santis rebounding and Chung and Slater teaming up with Chip in the fast break, the Statesmen swept forward for two more baskets to tie the score.

Assembly Hall broke out in pandemonium. The fans were yelling "Go SU! Go SU! Go! Go! Go!"

Chip turned slowly away from the Brandon players who had the ball out of bounds and took a step. Then he whirled back, intercepted the ball on the inbound pass, and laid it up to put State in the lead for the first time in the second half. The fans went wild! The momentum of the Statesmen increased as Chip led his teammates into a full-court man-to-man press. State scored two more quick buckets, and the Brandon players lost their poise. They began to travel with the ball, make bad passes, and take impossible shots. The result was a run of thirteen straight points for the Statesmen.

The fans were on their feet all the way, and the crowd noise grew in volume with each State University basket. Chip knew he and his teammates had pulled the game out of the fire, but he was surprised at the margin of victory. When the buzzer sounded and the game ended, they had succeeded: State 81, Brandon 72. The State bench emptied out on the floor and surrounded their starting five. They swept them off the court, out through the players' exit, and down to the locker room. Soapy and Speed got to Chip almost as soon as the buzzer ended the game.

"Thirty-nine!" Soapy shouted, slapping Chip on the back. "You got thirty-nine points!"

"You got ten in the last four minutes!" Speed yelled happily. "What a finish!"

It had taken a long time to get out in front, but the flurry of points at the end of the game had lifted the Statesmen's spirits, and the celebration intensified in the locker room. Their cheers and yells quieted only when Murph Kelly shouted for silence and gestured toward the doorway where Coach Stone stood silently viewing the scene.

"Let me have your attention," Stone said irritably. Waiting until the players quieted, he continued stiffly, "Well, you won, and that's *something*. But you didn't play good ball. Now you all listen, and listen good. Brandon was a pushover!

"But we don't have many pushovers on our schedule, and the first time you run up against a tough team, you're gonna need a system. *My* system! You all get this straight. You're going to play possession ball whether you like it or not. So when you report for practice Monday afternoon, I want you to know my offense inside and out. Does anyone here not have the outline?"

Looking around the stilled room, he frowned. "All right, get with it!" He waited a second and then turned and slammed the door shut behind him. A stunned silence followed Stone's departure. Then J. C. Tucker wadded up his warm-up jacket and threw it into his locker. "You would have thought we lost the game," he said bitterly.

Dom Di Santis said in a puzzled voice, "We win by nine, and he bawls us out. What's with that guy?"

"We *were* pretty ragged," Rudy Slater observed.

Speed Morris dropped a shoe heavily on the bottom of his locker. "Man, what does he expect in three days?" he demanded, looking around the room. "We can't learn a new style of play overnight."

Chip was in a hurry to get back to the store and did not join in the conversation. But he felt the same way his teammates did. The past few days had been hard to take. Stone's domineering manner and frenzied attempts to install his control offense had upset everyone. Chip was comforted by the thought that he and Soapy weren't on athletic scholarships. They could drop out of basketball, if necessary.

He didn't know much about coaching, but all the men for whom he had played before preferred to lead rather than drive. He knew his teammates well; they were real athletes and could take hard work. Stone seemed obsessed with a desire to reduce the team to absolute subjection, to control them as if they were a bunch of puppets. The Statesmen weren't used to such treatment, and their resentment had been growing ever since the first practice. *At least,* Chip thought bitterly, *Stone could express approval for the win.*

After all, it was a conference game. *Any* conference victory was important.

Soapy broke in on his thoughts. "Hurry up!"

"Where are you going?"

"With you! To the store! It's Saturday night, remember? I've got late curfew."

It was ten o'clock by the time Chip and Soapy reached the store and eleven before the last customer left and they could lock the doors. Soapy attended to some clean-up chores at the fountain, and Chip let Freeman out the front door and then carried the medication cases up to the office. He placed the boxes and the day's receipts in the safe, closed the big door, twirled the dial, and sat down wearily in Mr. Grayson's chair.

When Mitzi finished with her records, they closed the office, walked down the steps to the main floor, and waited until Soapy finished his work. Then Chip and Soapy walked Mitzi out through the main door and across the street to where her father was waiting in the employee parking lot.

"My car's in the shop," Mitzi explained. "Come on over and say hello to my dad."

A brisk, biting wind had sprung up, and Chip and Soapy gratefully accepted Mitzi's father's offer to drive them home. Mitzi got in the front seat beside her father as the flirting redhead moved to sit with Chip in the back. For the first few minutes of the drive, Soapy was unusually quiet but kept shifting around in the seat. Chip chuckled to himself. He could tell the redhead was dying to start a conversation. This was Soapy's big moment, and he wanted to make an impression on her father. Chip could sense the tremendous effort Soapy was making to think of something interesting to say, and he grinned in the darkness.

The streets were slippery, and the spinning wheels caused the car to slip sideways when Mr. Savrill pulled out of the parking lot. He drove slowly and carefully for a short distance and then told them he had seen the game.

This was Soapy's chance. "How did you like it?" he asked eagerly.

"I enjoyed the last five or six minutes."

"I'll bet you didn't like it when Chip and the guys kept passing the ball—"

"No, I can't say that I did, Soapy."

"You know how many times we're s'posed to pass the ball before we take a shot?" Soapy persisted.

"No, I don't."

"Ten times!" Soapy snorted. "Imagine playing walkathon basketball in this day and age!"

"The chief idea is to win, isn't it?" Mitzi asked.

"Sure!" Soapy agreed. "Of course."

"Well, then," Mitzi smiled over her shoulder, "what's the difference whether you run or walk?"

"Aw, Mitzi, it's not really like that," Soapy protested.

Mr. Savrill chuckled and braked the car to a stop in front of Jefferson Hall, and their conversation ended. Chip and Soapy thanked Mr. Savrill and said good night to Mitzi before running up the long walk to the porch. Inside it was warm and comfortable, and several dorm residents were talking in the reading room on the first floor. They shouted invitations to join them, but Chip and Soapy declined and hurried on up the steps to 212, their room on the second floor.

Chip wanted to do some studying, but he just couldn't. He was simply too tired. Reflecting that tomorrow was Sunday and he could spend quite a bit of time studying at the store, he decided against it and went to bed.

He was up early the next morning, but Soapy had beaten him. As usual, the redhead had gone out for the papers and some hot chocolate for Chip. He was back a little later. After reading the sports sections and discussing the front-page news, they rounded up Speed and the three friends went together to church. After services, Speed headed back to the dorm, while Chip and Soapy walked slowly down to Grayson's. Soapy had the evening off and left around six o'clock, but Chip worked straight through until closing time.

Grayson's closed at nine o'clock on Sunday evenings. Chip closed up on time, but he had to wait until Cara Davis finished her records. She was new at the job and didn't complete her work until ten o'clock, and it was ten-thirty before he reached Jeff. Then, despite Soapy's protests, he studied until midnight.

The Valley Falls crowd met each school day for lunch at the cafeteria in the student union. Since he had no afternoon classes on Monday, Chip decided to visit with his friends before going on to Grayson's. Soapy, Speed, Biggie, and Red were at their favorite table avidly discussing Stone's possession offense. They took time off to greet him and then went right back to the discussion. Chip sat down and listened.

"How come so many teams are using it?" Biggie demanded.

"Because it's a fad," Soapy announced.

"How about it, Chip?" Biggie asked.

"Soapy's right, in a way," Chip said. "Some of the big-name teams like Southwestern, Western, and A & M use the control game and win with it. A lot of teams copy them."

"Southwestern won the national championship playing control ball," Speed observed.

"Yeah," Soapy added, rising and picking up his books, "and now we're using it."

"Don't overlook Northern State," Chip said slowly. "That's what they beat us with in the Garden."

"Sure!" Speed added, "Plus pushing, elbowing, holding, and tripping."

"Brannon's teams always play that way," Soapy growled. "I'm surprised Stone hasn't tried to teach us the same kind of junk."

"Well," Biggie said, pushing himself up and away from the table, "I've got a class. See you later."

Biggie's motion broke up the meeting. They all walked out of the building and parted to go their separate ways. Chip walked down to Grayson's and worked until 2:30. Then he took off for practice.

Coach Stone held a strategy session before the workout that afternoon and asked each player to go to the white board, draw the formations and plays, and then discuss the control game. The procedure was new to the Statesmen, but most of them were ready. However, Jimmy Chung and Branch Phillips were unprepared and caught the full blast of Stone's anger. He kept them at the board until they knew the system by heart, throwing question after question at them.

Branch stood seven feet in height, while Jimmy had to hold himself as straight as a broomstick to reach ten inches over five feet. The difference in their heights presented an incongruous picture, and their confusion and embarrassment as a result of Stone's hammering drew a strong feeling of sympathy from their teammates. It was over at last, but the Statesmen's pizzazz and enthusiasm had evaporated by the time Stone at last sent them out on the court.

Stone devoted the rest of the workout to the Western scouting notes. It was six o'clock when he called it a day. And, once again, he asked Chip to remain behind. When the last player left the court, Stone sat down beside Chip and began to talk.

"We've got a big job on our hands next Saturday," he said, looking steadily at Chip. "Western is a tough team, and it's up to you to keep our control game on an even keel, but that isn't what I wanted us to talk about. I want to talk about you."

"Me?"

"That's right. I don't like the way you've been acting during the workouts."

CHAPTER 8

Working Is a Hobby

"ACTING!" Chip repeated. "What—"

Coach Mike Stone held up a hand and continued, "I don't mean you're not putting out, Hilton. It's just that you're not sharp. You're tired. Right?"

Chip nodded. "Yes, sir, I guess I am."

Stone shook his head slowly. The lines of his face were tight and the set of his jaw was grim. "I don't get it. On a scholarship you could quit working and concentrate on your studies and basketball. And," he added, "you could do it in a breeze. *Your* way, it isn't possible. You're doing too much. School has to come first. I'm sure your mother sent you here to get an education, not to work all night in a drugstore."

Chip was thinking he was also getting a very good, practical education at Grayson's, but he said nothing. Stone waited a few moments and then continued.

"What about the responsibilities you have to the school and basketball? Aren't they important?"

"Yes, sir, of course they are. But the store is important, too, especially now."

"You've won the national basketball shooting tournament two times in a row. How are you going to find time for that?"

"I'm not going to enter this year."

"Well, how about your responsibilities as captain of the team and as an all-American player? And what about your teammates? Don't you think you owe them some loyalty?"

Chip nodded. "Of course I do, sir. That's one of the reasons I'm sticking with the team."

Stone eyed Chip speculatively and then shook his head in defeat. "I don't think you can keep going this way, Hilton. And I don't see how I can give you any more privileges."

"I don't expect any privileges, Coach. I'll make it."

Stone rose slowly to his feet. "Well," he said heavily, "I certainly hope so. Good night."

Beginning with Tuesday morning, each day seemed one long succession of classes, work, basketball practice, studying, writing papers, opening the store in the morning, checking at noon, and closing up at night.

And at practice, Mike Stone hammered and hammered at the players each afternoon, driving them without letup from the moment they reported right up to the last second of the workout. The players took it, but they didn't like it, and Chip could tell that little by little team morale was fading.

He did his best to rally his teammates' spirits. He forced himself to set the example and led the drills at full speed. He hustled and fought in each practice and scrimmage as hard as if it were a game.

At the end of each practice, he felt drained of every bit of his strength. Some evenings he could scarcely muster enough energy to walk to Grayson's. It showed up in his work, and Soapy summed it all up correctly on Friday when he woke up at two in the morning to find Chip still studying at his desk.

The redhead sat up in bed and regarded Chip with the disgust that often accompanies worry. "C'mon, Chip!" he pleaded. "Go to bed. What are you trying to do, kill yourself?"

"I can't fall behind in my course work."

"Huh!" Soapy grunted. "Everything is *can't* with you! You *can't* fall behind in your grades, you *can't* let Mr. Grayson down, you *can't* quit school, and you *can't* quit basketball. Well, I know you *can't* keep up this kind of a life very long."

Soapy got up from his bed, closed Chip's science books with a determined snap, and turned out the light. "There!" he said shortly, "If you have to stay up, sit up in the dark. At least you'll give your eyes a rest."

Someone was pounding on the door and a voice was saying something and there was some sort of buzzing, but it took a long time for the words to register. Then the door opened, and Ted Brown, one of the guys on Chip's floor, snapped off the clock radio and peered down at him.

"Hey! Chip! Wake up. Your phone's been ringing on and off for ten solid minutes!"

Chip glanced at the clock and his mind came wide awake. "Oh, no!" he groaned. "Nine o'clock! Soapy must have forgotten to set the alarm."

"He set it," Brown said. "I just turned it off! I don't know how you slept through that buzzer *and* the phone!"

"I didn't hear it," Chip moaned, throwing back the covers. "I didn't hear anything at all! I must have been sound asleep."

"You mean *dead*," Brown said, looking at him curiously. "You better start getting some sleep, Chip."

Chip thanked Brown, threw on jeans and a sweater, and pulled on his jacket. Just as he was heading out the door, the phone rang again.

It was Soapy and the redhead was breathless and upset. "Chip! What's the matter? We can't get in the store! We've been waiting outside for half an hour. Welch is ready to explode, and the rest of us are half-frozen. What happened?"

"I overslept, Soapy. Isn't Mr. Dixon there?"

"This is Saturday, remember? Dixon doesn't come in until noon, and Mitzi doesn't either. No one else has a key."

"Where are you calling from?"

"Pete's place. I've got Fireball's car. I'll be right there."

"I'll be out front."

Chip had just bounded down the front steps when Soapy pulled into the driveway in Fireball's Volkswagen bug. Chip jumped in.

"I set the alarm for eight o'clock," Soapy said, his freckled nose scrunching up in confusion. "Didn't it go off?"

"It went off," Chip said grimly.

"Did you go back to sleep?"

"No, Soapy. I never even heard it."

"What about the phone? I called about five times!"

"I didn't hear that either."

"See!" Soapy snapped. "That's what I was trying to tell you last night. You're bushed. I bet you've never slept through an alarm or a phone before in your life."

"No, I guess not."

Soapy eyed Chip with concern and then warned him. "Man, Chip, Welch is upset. You'd better steer clear of him today."

"Listen, Soapy, I don't care how Welch feels. Now will you just let it rest? I overslept! Period!"

Chip regretted his words and the tone of voice he used as soon as the comment escaped his lips. *What's the matter with me?* he asked himself. *Why am I talking to Soapy like that?*

The conversation ended there. Chip was angry with himself. Soapy stared quietly out the front window and carefully navigated the snowy, icy streets. The clock over Grayson's main door showed 9:15 when they piled out of the car. Kurt Welch, Cara Davis, Skip Miller, Lonnie Freeman, Fireball Finley, and two or three other employees were standing in front of the store, stamping their feet and penguining their arms to keep warm.

Chip hurried up the walk to the entrance. "I'm sorry, everyone," he said apologetically. "It's my fault. I overslept. It won't happen again."

"Oh, don't worry about us," Welch said sarcastically. "We'll get used to your methods of running the business in time. Anyway, working is just a hobby with *us*."

"I said I was sorry," Chip said shortly. He held the door open for Cara and then continued on through the store.

Behind him he heard Welch comment again, speaking just loud enough for Chip to hear: "You have to get used to things like this when someone sends a boy to do a man's job."

A feeling of resentment hit the top of Chip's chest like a hammer. He stopped in his tracks. It took all of his self-control to hold himself in check. He realized he was tired and upset, and he knew angry words now would only result in further resentment and regret later. So he ignored the taunt, went upstairs to the office, and hustled into his work, trying to force Welch out of his mind.

His duties kept him moving between the office and the stockroom most of the day, but whenever he passed through the store, he heard remarks about the conference race and the game with Western scheduled for that night.

In the stockroom, just before he and Soapy started out for Assembly Hall, Chip grasped the redhead by the arm. "Listen, Soapy," he said awkwardly, "I—"

"Hold *everything*," Soapy said quickly. "You don't ever have to explain anything to me. You know that. Our friendship can withstand a little stress, Chip."

"Yes," Chip said, grinning, "I guess I do. Anyway, well, let's get going."

They matched long strides up Main Street and along State's broad campus walks. When Chip and Soapy reached Assembly Hall's big trophy foyer, classmates, friends, and fans instantly spotted them and moved to make a path so they could pass through. Soapy led the way through the crowd, nodding and speaking to everyone.

"Hi, Chip. How ya doing, Soapy?"

"How many points tonight, Chip? Seventy-two?"

"This is a conference game, Hilton. Ya gotta win it!"

Chip smiled and nodded at the fans but didn't say anything. Soapy, however, fired replies right and left as they milled through the crowd.

"We'll kill 'em!"

"It's a done deal!"

"Leave everything to me and Chip."

"Nothing to it!"

They were the last of the Statesmen to arrive. The two quickly changed into their crisp white jerseys and their red, white, and blue State University warm-ups.

Murph Kelly was working on Di Santis's knee. Chip sat down on the bench in front of his locker and tried to relax. Coach Stone paced back and forth across the locker room, but when Kelly finished with Dom, the coach stopped his stride and clapped his hands together to gain their attention.

"Everyone over here!" he said sharply, gesturing toward the rows of benches in front of the white board. He waited until they were settled and then looked at the trainer. "How much time?"

"Thirty-five minutes to game time, Coach," Kelly said shortly.

"Good. We've got time to review our strategy. Give me ten minutes."

Kelly nodded and checked his watch. Stone turned back to the players. "All right, now," he said briskly. "Let's get organized. You've been working against Western's fast break and their screening attack a solid week. Right?" Stone's jaw was firm, and his dark brown eyes seemed even darker as they bore into the face of each player.

His intense attitude expressed the tremendous effort he applied to his coaching, and the sheer power of his personality forced each player to nod in agreement.

"Remember," he continued, "they like to run and they like to shoot. Even when their break is slowed down and you force them into a set formation, they hurry their shots. I want you to stop their fast break and then use your control game to slow them down some more. All right, Chung, you tell us how we're going to stop their fast break."

Jimmy grimaced and got slowly to his feet. "Well," he said slowly, "we're supposed to pass the ball a lot. That takes up time. When we take a shot, three of us are supposed to follow in. And we've got to make sure two of us are back all the time on defense—" Jimmy paused and scratched his head.

"Go on," Stone urged. "What about the rebounder?"

Jimmy nodded. "Oh, that's right! Well, one of us is supposed to guard him and try to keep him from making the outlet pass."

"And—" Stone prompted.

"And the backcourt players are supposed to guard the possible receivers of the outlet passes so the rebounder won't be able to get rid of the ball."

"Good!" Stone interjected. "You take it from there, Morris."

Speed stood up, sure and confident. "Next," he said quickly, "we're supposed to stop the man with the ball, the dribbler. Then anyone who hasn't done one of the assignments Jimmy mentioned drops back—"

"*Runs!*"

"*Runs* back," Speed repeated. "Runs back *as fast* as he can to set up the shuttle defense."

"That's enough!" Stone said. His eyes ranged over the players until they settled on Rudy Slater. "You put that on the white board and explain it, Slater."

Slater quickly drew four rough court outlines on the board and then lined in the moves of the players.

When he finished the drawings, Slater faced his teammates and began his explanation of the shuttle. "Well," he

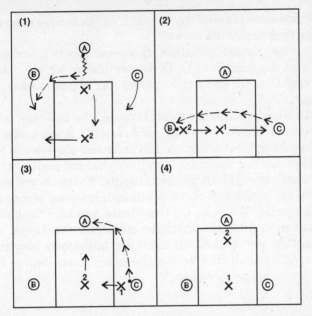

said slowly, "in the first situation, players A, B, and C are Western players who have a three-on-two situation going against us. Defensive players 1 and 2, that's us, are set up with X1 on the free-throw line and X2 under the basket."

"What's the chief purpose of this shuttle defense?" Stone interrupted.

"To keep the area under the basket covered at all times," Slater answered.

"And what else?"

"Well, to keep A, B, and C from scoring, or at least to hold them until the rest of the defensive players can get back to help out."

Stone nodded. "Right. *Everyone* hustles back when we lose the ball."

"In the first situation," Slater continued, "player X1 is supposed to stop the dribbler and force him to pass the ball to B or C. Here, A passes to B. As soon as A passes the ball to B, defensive player X2 covers him and defensive player X1 drops back under the basket.

"In the second situation, B passes the ball across in front of the basket to C. Defensive player X1 now starts toward C, and defensive player X2 drops under the basket.

"In situation number three, C passes the ball back out to A. Now X2 breaks out to guard A, and X1 drops under the basket. In the last situation, the defensive players are back in their starting alignment but have changed positions."

"That's enough!" Stone said bitingly. "Everyone got that?"

No one spoke and Stone continued, his voice strong and commanding. "All right. On the offense, you hold the ball for a sure shot. After the shot, you stop their fast break. And when they set up their offensive formation, you play them tight. And you all stick with it the entire game—win or lose. *But you're not going to lose!*"

CHAPTER 9

Control Game

MIKE STONE'S sheer confidence and intense desire to win got through to the Statesmen for the first time. The fierce fury of his determination now gripped them, too, and they couldn't wait for him to name the starting lineup. Chip was stirred by Stone's words, and a new sense of power surged through him. He could make it. *He had to make it!*

The shock of Stone's rasping voice broke through his thoughts. "Hilton! Di Santis! Slater! Phillips! Chung! Let's go!"

As his teammates followed Chip out onto their home court, the fans' encouraging cheers and the jazz band's thundering rendition of State's victory march added to Chip's feeling of strength. This was all he needed, he told himself during the warm-up drills. A guy might get tired from working and studying, but it was a different kind of fatigue. He could never get tired of basketball!

The Statesmen played Stone's slow-down control game to the letter. They forgot all about their fast break and concentrated on good passes, good screens, and good shots. Chip and Jimmy would advance slowly to the front court with the ball, screen for one another, and play catch until Phillips took his position in the outer half of the free-throw circle and Di Santis and Slater had time to move to the corners.

When their teammates were set, Chip or Jimmy would start the four-man weave with Di Santis and Slater and pass and screen and pass and screen until one of their Western opponents made a dive for the ball. Then it was a fast cut, a pass, and a quick shot. Chip and Chung took most of the shots and did most of the scoring.

On the defense, they conscientiously applied the methods Stone had planned to stop Western's famed fast break, and the strategy worked! Western simply couldn't get their fast break into high gear, and State forced them to play their new game.

Both teams were geared for fast-paced basketball action, and neither team was expert in the use of the control-ball offense. As a result, the players became overcautious. The results were deliberate passing and cutting and extremely slow action. The State fans didn't like it, but it was early and the score was close, so they encouraged the Statesmen with solid cheers and applause.

About ten minutes into the first half, Chip took three shots and missed them all. It was hard to understand. The shots were short jumpers, about fifteen feet from the basket, and he felt confident each time. But the ball didn't swish through the net.

Minutes later, Chip again broke free from the Western player who was dogging him. This time, the smooth flow of power surging up from the ankles through his body, shoulder, elbow, wrist, and fingers was missing. Once again, his shot was off line, bouncing off the ring and right into the hands of a Western rebounder.

So far into the game, Chip had covered his opponent expertly. He had anticipated every move the Western player attempted and had shut him out from the field. But suddenly, inexplicably, his moves became sluggish and his opponent cut past him for two quick baskets. Now he was worried; he realized there was more than staleness slowing him down.

The harder he tried, the more erratic his play became. To make it worse, his teammates began to make all sorts of misplays. They traveled with the ball, dribbled too much, fumbled, and made bad passes. During this disastrous demonstration, the Western players managed to maintain their poise and capitalize on each mistake. They advanced six points out in front.

Now the fans' support faltered. This wasn't the kind of basketball they had come to see. They wanted action—hard running, daring passes, driving plays, and spectacular shots.

"What are you waiting for, State?"

"C'mon, Hilton! Open up!"

"Go SU! Go SU! Go! Go! Go! SU!"

Chip heard the crowd and tried to speed it up, tried to break free with his usual finesse. But his teammates were now grooved in the control game, and his efforts upset their passing rhythm. The result was a bad pass, which he fumbled. To make it worse, a Western opponent recovered the ball and dribbled the length of the court to score with an unguarded layup. That put Western eight points ahead. Stone called time.

Chip glanced at the scoreboard. Visitors 34, State 26, with four minutes left to play in the half.

Stone's face was hard and set when the players circled him in front of the bench. He glanced keenly at Chip and then jerked a thumb over his shoulder. "Take a rest, Hilton," he said sharply. "Tucker! You're in for Hilton."

Chip rode the bench for the rest of the half, and when he followed his teammates off the court, the big scoreboard showed the low score: Visitors 38, State 28.

Murph Kelly checked their ankles and probed for injuries while Andre Gilbert passed out Gatorade and oranges. When they were finished, Stone took over. "What an exhibition!" he barked. "Control basketball means just that—*control* the basketball! You must have thrown it away twenty times!"

Disgust was etched into his set expression. He turned away and took several strides back and forth. Suddenly he wheeled and pointed a finger at each of the starters. "You, Hilton, Di Santis, Phillips, Slater, and Chung—you're quitting on your school and your teammates and on me! *Quitting cold!*"

Mike Stone pounded the table with his fist again and again until the table jumped and rattled under the force. His face was a mottled red and white, and the locker room light reflected sharply off his dark eyes like sparklers on a Fourth of July evening. "You've lost your poise and your confidence and you're letting a second-rate, run-and-shoot ball club beat you at your own game.

"Where's your fight? Where's your pride? And, where's your guts?"

A cold fury had been building up through Chip as he listened to the tirade. No coach had ever talked to him this way. *What was wrong with Stone?*

The angry coach paced back and forth several times and then picked up a ball and twirled it in his hands. "All right, Hilton," he said harshly, "take Di Santis, Slater, Chung, and Phillips back out on that court and give the people who came here to see basketball something for their money."

He looked along the row of faces and then tossed the ball into Chip's hands. "Let's go!" he said roughly.

Chip caught the ball and slowly rose to his feet. Stone seemed to have lost all sense of decency. A real coach didn't talk that way to his players. And, he reflected, a player with pride couldn't take that kind of talk. For a moment he hesitated, fighting back the urge to toss the ball away and quit basketball right then and there.

Then cold logic took over, and he thrust aside his anger. He wasn't going to quit something he loved because of pride. Besides, he was the captain, and his teammates looked to him for leadership. They resented Stone's words as much as he did, and he could sense their anger and disquiet. They were ready to stampede and would follow him, no matter what the consequences, if he made the first move. But a player didn't quit under fire, no matter how much it hurt.

He turned and led his teammates through the door and along the hall to the players' ramp and out onto the court. The crowd roar caught him up, and he dribbled out to the State basket and tried to forget his anger by concentrating on his warm-up shots. With each shot, a degree of tension lifted, and five minutes later, when the referee blew his whistle, most of Chip's anger had evaporated.

The fans were behind the Statesmen once more. This was a new half; now was the time to get going! Four male cheerleaders ran up and down the length of the court, proudly waving large red and white State University banners that rippled and fluttered with the movement. The jazz band, moving in joy to the rhythm of their own music, brandished their trumpets first to the right, then to the left, and the bass drum reverberated to the rafters, blending in with the spectators' cheers.

And when the opposing team inbounded the ball to start the second half, the fans were once again chanting "Go SU! Go SU! Go SU!"

Jimmy got enough of his hand on the inbound to deflect it, and Chip got the ball. This time he hustled into the front court and got the offense moving. Yes, the Statesmen were still using Stone's control game, but there was a fresh zip to their passes and moves, and the period was less than ten seconds gone when Chip scored with a jumper from behind one of Jimmy Chung's screens.

The halftime rest had helped Chip, but it took only a few minutes of game action for him to discover that his muscles were still tired and that he had once again lost his spark. He was played out, and for as far back as he could remember, this was the first time he had wished a game were over. He gave it all he had, but it just wasn't enough.

Stone took him out of the game for another rest. "Sit down, Hilton," Stone said with concern. "If you don't get some rest one way or another pretty soon, you're going to end up in the hospital."

The words erased Chip's resentment toward the coach, and when Stone sent him back in the last ten minutes of the game, he was determined to go all out if he fell flat on his face. He glanced at the scoreboard. *Six points down and ten minutes to go.*

It was State's ball out of bounds under their own basket, and Jimmy passed to Chip and cut on ahead to give him a chance to dribble into the front court. Chip had intended to set up the weave, but his opponent had dropped off and was waiting deep, toward the basket. Chip stopped and took a long shot just inside the three-point line, and it hit. Now the Statesmen were only four points behind.

With Chip back in the game, the Statesmen stiffened on the defense and held Western scoreless for three minutes. During this interim Chung scored twice, and with the score tied, the teams began to trade baskets.

Chip's teammates now began to look to him for the sure shot, the automatic two points, and for the first time since he had reported for basketball at the start of the season, Chip was afraid to shoot. He kept passing off.

Jimmy, Dom, and Rudy scored to keep pace with the Western team. There was less than a minute left to play with the score still tied.

With the end of the game in sight, tempers flared and the game developed into a bitter dog fight. Chung dribbled free for a score, but Western came right back to even it up. It was State's ball and Chip decided to hold it for one shot. He gave the freeze signal and drew on every ounce of his reserve strength to battle through the stretch.

CONTROL GAME

With tension at a feverish pitch and less than ten seconds left to play, he broke free for a shot. His first thought was to go up for a jumper, but he remembered the misses and drove on in for a layup. A frantic Western opponent tried desperately to stop the shot and fouled him, but Chip had released the ball and it zipped through the ring and the net to break the tie and put State out in front by a single bucket.

There were only seconds left to play when Chip dropped in the free throw to put the Statesmen ahead by three points. Western tried a long desperation shot after the inbound, but the attempt was wide of the basket and the game was over. The final score: State 79, Western 76.

Chip had forgotten Stone's halftime tirade during the hectic last ten minutes of the game, but it came flooding back as he moved along toward the locker room. Then a bit of doubt started to tumble around in his mind. Despite the fact that Western had double-teamed him and tried everything in the playbook to stop his scoring, Chip knew what had been responsible for the Statesmen's near loss of the game—he'd lost his shooting touch. And, grudgingly, he had to admit that State probably would have lost the game if Stone had not fired the Statesmen up to such a fighting pitch.

The Statesmen were jubilant and boisterous when they bounded into the locker room, but they quieted when they saw Stone half-standing, half-sitting on the trainers' table. Andre Gilbert and campus security kept the fans waiting outside and closed the door when the last player entered. Then Stone began to speak.

"You played a good game, and I want to congratulate every player in the room. You showed that you could fight and come from behind to win, and that's the mark of a good team.

"I was a little rough on you between the halves, and if I hurt anyone's feelings, I'm sorry. However, I felt it was the only way to pull you together.

"Now, starting next Friday with College of the West, we play three conference teams in a row, all at home. We play Mercer on Saturday and Eastern the following Saturday. If we can win all three of these games, it will put us right on A & M's heels where we belong. See you Monday at three o'clock sharp. Good night."

There was a tight silence for a moment or two after Andre closed the door behind Stone. Then, somewhat uncertainly at first, the victory celebration resumed. Chip noticed that Di Santis, Slater, and Chung didn't join in with the rest of their teammates. They dressed quietly and were lost in the crowd of fans who tried to press into the locker room when Andre opened the door.

Chip didn't know what to think or do. As team captain, he knew it was his responsibility to talk to Stone on behalf of the players if he thought it was necessary. But he thrust the thought aside. Right then he was more interested in getting back to Grayson's and closing the store so he could get a good night's sleep.

CHAPTER 10

Worse Than a Quitter

SOAPY SMITH'S bed was already neatly made, and the red-head was gone when Chip woke up Sunday morning. But that was his regular routine. The redhead was the first Jeff student up and about on *any* day, and this morning was no exception. His usual Sunday morning routine was to wake up exactly five minutes before the alarm clock was set to ring, dress, and make his bed while Chip slept. Then he would tiptoe out of the room and jog down one of the bike paths to a small convenience store.

At the store, Soapy would pick up some sandwiches or doughnuts and hot chocolate and then walk briskly back to Jefferson Hall and up the dormitory's broad front steps. Today, balancing a bag filled with hot chocolate and doughnuts in one hand, he swooped up two of the Sunday news-papers—the *Herald* and the *News*—stacked in two large bundles on the front porch of the large brick dormitory. And, somehow, his timing was just right, with him returning soon after Chip had awakened.

Chip stretched his muscles and then relaxed a moment as he reviewed the previous night. Stone had poured it on the team, but the more Chip thought about it, the more he was forced to admit that there had been some justification. He and his teammates had started out full of determination, but they had wilted, especially in the first half when Western forced the pace.

His own play had been substandard from the beginning, he reflected. It wasn't staleness; he wasn't practicing and playing too much basketball. He was just tired out from burning the candle at both ends. He smiled ruefully. He had heard that expression all his life, but for the first time he understood—really understood!—what it meant. A guy simply couldn't get up early in the morning, go to work or classes, keep going all day, practice basketball, work all evening, study late at night, and then expect to feel good. He just wasn't getting enough rest.

If he could only find a little extra time to study during the day, he could go right to bed when he got home at night. He was carrying only fifteen hours, but all his subjects were tough. As it was, he spent every bit of his spare time studying. The only thing he could possibly quit was basketball.

Quit! *Quit* was a nasty word. He didn't like it. Then, suddenly, he remembered a sports axiom Coach Rockwell had posted in the Valley Falls High School gymnasium: Worse Than a Quitter—Someone Who Won't Try.

That did it! At least he could try. He was up to his neck in school and Grayson's and basketball, and this was no time to feel sorry for himself. State had the team to go all the way, and he was the captain. It was his job to lead and fight, and he was going to do it! He was going to give all he had and more, even if he had to do it dribbling in his sleep!

It was cold, and he had showered after the game the night before, but he figured another quick plunge might shock some of the lethargy out of his muscles. Without letting himself reconsider, he leaped out of bed and headed straight for the shower. It was a real shocker, but by the time he got back to the room, he felt good.

Soapy was sprawled out on his bed reading the *News*. He had set the doughnuts and hot chocolate on Chip's desk and spread the *Herald* sports page over the top of Chip's books. "There!" he said briskly. "The pause that refreshes."

He came over and pointed to the *Herald* headline. "See that?" he demanded. Without waiting for Chip's answer, Soapy read the headline.

A & M LEADS CONFERENCE RACE
WITH SEVEN STRAIGHT WINS

"We're in second place," Chip said, "right?"

"No. Third place. Northern State is second. They're six and zero. We're five and one. Read it!"

> A & M's high-flying Aggies are in first place as a result of seven straight conference victories. Northern State notched their fourth consecutive victory last night, demolishing Eastern 79-54. It was their twelfth win in thirteen starts. The Northerners' only defeat was a loss to the national title holder, Southwestern, in the finals of the Holiday Invitational Tournament.
>
> No doubt, all of us remember that our local Statesmen lost to Northern State in the semifinal round by a mere two points, 83-81. . . .

Soapy tapped the paper with his finger. "Coach Brannon won *that* game."

"When he kicked the ball?"

"That's right!" Soapy said belligerently. "It was our ball, and he killed at least ten seconds. If he hadn't done that, you would have had time to get that last shot away, and you were open and right under the basket! How come the officials let him pull that?"

"They must not have seen him do it."

"Well, I bet everyone else in the Garden saw it," Soapy said angrily. "Some coach!"

"The season isn't over," Chip said. "We play them twice more at home. I just hope I—"

"Can last," Soapy finished for his friend. "Right?"

"I'll last," Chip replied, his jaw tightening.

"Maybe," Soapy said. "Wait a minute. I want you to see what Jim Locke wrote in his column in the *News*."

Soapy leafed through the paper until he came to the sports pages and Jim Locke's column. Then he spread the paper on the desk. "There!" he said, pointing to a paragraph halfway down the column. "Read that!"

> State University squeaked through a bitter battle last night against Western to win by a three-point margin. Hilton's driving layup and free throw made the win in the last seconds of the game. Despite last night's victory and the nine-point defeat of Brandon a week earlier, the Statesmen are far below national rating consideration and doubtful contenders for conference honors.

Soapy regarded Chip solemnly. "How do you like that?" he demanded.

"I don't."

"You're going to like the rest of it less. Go on, read it."

> State students and fans watched in shocked disbelief as the mighty Statesmen committed 26 floor errors during the game. To further add to their dismay, the usually reliable Chip Hilton had one of his few bad nights. The fans couldn't believe their eyes during one stage of the game when Hilton missed four straight shots less than fifteen feet from the basket.

"He's right," Chip said. "I was terrible."

"There were others," Soapy said dryly. "Oh, another thing. Kinser is in first place in the national scoring race. He got fifty-one points last night to boost his average to 43.1. Your average is 42. It's right here in the paper."

"Good for him. What do you say we hit the books, Soapy? We've both got tests coming up."

Soapy groaned. "I know, I know." He paused, grinned, and then added tritely, "But not very *much*."

They studied until 10:30 and then went to church. After the services, Soapy went back to Jeff to study, and Chip went downtown to open the store. He managed to get in some studying during the afternoon and then called Mrs. Grayson. "Yes, Chip, Mr. Grayson is doing fine," she said. After the call, he told the rest of the staff the news about Mr. Grayson and went back to his books.

Business was slow, and it was a relief to close up at nine o'clock and head back to Jeff. Soapy had studied all day and took off for a walk as soon as Chip arrived. He was back in half an hour, and that night, for the first time in nearly two weeks, they were both asleep by eleven o'clock.

The days that followed were much alike. Chip followed his regular routine religiously: wake up at 7:30, open the store, remain until he had to leave for a class, return for lunch, come back for classes and practice, go back to work, and then head home to Jeff and his books. It was sheer drudgery—boring, plodding, tedious, even grueling at times.

But just when he felt he couldn't stand it any longer, Mrs. Grayson would call with the news that Mr. Grayson was steadily improving. That would cheer him up, and he would go back to work with renewed vigor.

Twice during the week Mrs. Grayson dropped by the store to visit. She told Chip Mr. Grayson was enjoying his forced "vacation" and that he was delighted with the operation of the store. "Is there anything I can do to help?" she asked.

"No, Mrs. Grayson, everything's fine."

"That's what Mitzi says. Everyone thinks you're doing a

wonderful job. It seems to me as if Mr. Grayson has been gone a month."

Chip nodded and smiled. It seemed more like a year to him, but he wasn't going to let Mrs. Grayson know that.

Mrs. Grayson studied his face for a moment. "Are you sure you aren't overdoing things?" she asked. "You look tired and pale, Chip."

"I'm all right, Mrs. Grayson. Right now I'm doing a lot of studying, that's all."

After Mrs. Grayson left, Chip managed to put in an hour on his books. Then, on the way to practice, he thought back to the tongue-lashing Stone had given the team at halftime in the Western game. His teammates had disliked it as much as he had. They had grumbled about it, but no one had been insolent. Chip guessed they were in the same boat with Soapy and himself. All of them were too busy going to classes, practicing basketball, and studying to think much about anything else.

Friday night brought the first of three straight conference games. College of the West put up a stubborn battle, but the Statesmen got out in front in the first minute of play and held that position all the way to the final buzzer.

Stone substituted freely, even though the game was close all the way through. He experimented with Speed, J. C. Tucker, and Bitsy Reardon in an obvious effort to find someone who could assume the responsibility of the play making. But he finished with the starting five. The final score: State 67, College of the West, 63.

Saturday night, Stone and the Statesmen ran head-on into a surprise and near defeat. Mercer put an undersized team of hustlers on the court and ran the Statesmen breathless. Mercer's tallest player was six-four, Chip's height, but the team made up for their lack of height with fight and pressure. Their offense and defense were the same, a continuous advance toward the basket with the use of pressure every second of the game.

Mercer lined up for the game-opening tap on a matched man-to-man basis and stuck to their assigned Statesmen like peanut butter on bread, except when one broke free to score.

State's control game never did get organized. In fact, the Statesmen seldom had a chance to get to their front-court positions. Chip and Jimmy were the only two players on the starting five who were good enough dribblers and ball handlers to keep the ball away from the eager opponents, and Stone sent J. C. Tucker, Speed Morris, and Bitsy Reardon in for Di Santis, Slater, and Phillips. The teams were evenly matched in height with this lineup, but it was the first time these players had been assembled as a team, and it took three-quarters of the game for them to get used to working together.

It was a wild contest of frenzied action, bad passes, diving interceptions, and desperate shots. The fans got caught up in the fever of the action and cheered and yelled and groaned and tried to lend a hand in every play with their arms, legs, and bodies.

Chip had been in the game all the way and scored repeatedly, but it didn't stop the visitors. With less than three minutes left to play, the Statesmen were eleven points behind. Chip never did figure out where he got the strength, but with every person in Assembly Hall standing and cheering him on—students, fans, teammates, and coaches—he scored nine straight points to bring the Statesmen within two points of the visitors. Then, with seven seconds left to play, it was his ten-foot jump shot that tied the score and sent the game into overtime.

In the extra period, he added seven more points to climax his spectacular point surge and lead the Statesmen to a three-point victory. The final score: State 79, Mercer 76.

The fans were on the court almost as soon as the buzzer ended the game. They wanted to share in the victory with the players. But Chip and his teammates quickly broke for the locker room, anxious to get away from the scene of the hectic game.

Chip had felt tired enough to sit right down on the court. But he had forced himself to hustle off the floor and through the players' exit to the sanctuary of Murph Kelly's locker room. He sank down on the bench in front of his locker, out of breath, with perspiration oozing from every pore in his body and every muscle aching. He was completely exhausted, but he was now also fired up with the certainty that he and his teammates could win, no matter what kind of an offense they used.

Kelly came over and lifted him to his feet. "Get in the shower," he said roughly. "Now! And then get back here to the trainers' table."

Chip quickly showered and had just hopped up on the table when Coach Stone reached the room. Stone walked over to the table and looked inquisitively at the trainer. "Anything wrong?" he asked.

"No," Kelly said. "He just needs a little rubdown."

"I'm all right," Chip broke in. "This is Murph's idea."

"It's a good one," Stone said. He shook his head and breathed a deep sigh of relief. "What a travesty! If that was basketball, I'm a sewing teacher."

Tired as he was, the unlikely picture of big Mike Stone holding a tiny needle in his hamlike hands was funny, and Chip couldn't resist a grin. Stone caught the smile, and his set expression relaxed as he glanced around the room. Some of the players had stopped dressing when he came in, but most of them had kept right on. Stone waited a second and then addressed Kelly and Andre Gilbert. "No practice until Wednesday."

That shocked the Statesmen out of their lethargy and silence. An involuntary cheer sounded from everyone. A quick smile crept across Stone's lips. He looked down at Chip. "*You,*" he said, tapping him on the chest, "get some rest. Good night."

CHAPTER 11

On the
National Scene

CHIP LEAFED through the pages he had written and carefully reread each of his responses. Satisfied with his proofreading, he closed the test pamphlet, got to his feet, and walked quietly to the front of the room. He dropped the blue book in the basket on Professor Connolly's desk.

It was a warm, sunny day, and the thin layer of snow on the walk was just beginning to melt. He walked slowly across the campus and down Main Street, enjoying the rare experience of being able to relax, to actually take time going somewhere. It was the first time in weeks he didn't have to worry about rushing to a class, Grayson's, or a practice. He was finished with his last test for the week. Now there was nothing to worry about except Grayson's and basketball.

Chip felt pretty good about the basketball picture. A & M and Northern State were running one-two in the conference standings, but State was marching right behind them. The two home games with them would settle the issue. Winning the conference might mean an invitation to the NCAA Tournament—March Madness!

He purchased a copy of the *News* out of a machine on the corner, tucked it under his arm, and continued on to Grayson's. A stack of his books was piled on top of Mr. Grayson's desk, but he pushed them aside and sat down in his employer's leather swivel chair. He was tired, but he felt a great sense of satisfaction.

All his studying had paid off. He felt confident he had done well on his tests. And he had earned an *A* on his twentieth-century history paper. It was quiet in the office. He put his head down on his arms, closed his eyes, and relaxed completely.

The intercom on the desk buzzed several times before Chip woke with a start. It took him a moment or so to realize that he had been sound asleep. He snapped the button and answered.

"What have you been doing up there, sleeping?" Soapy laughed.

Chip laughed. "Believe it or not," he said, "that's *just* what I've been doing. What time is it?"

"Time to go to practice."

"Be right with you."

Soapy was talking to Cara Davis at the cashier's desk, and reluctantly followed him out of the store.

"How did you make out with your statistics exam?" Chip asked.

"All right, I hope, I hope," Soapy said cheerfully. "Think of it! No major assignments for at least a week!"

"We've got four games to play," Chip reminded his friend.

"We'll kill 'em!"

"I don't know about that. Carlton beat us before . . . on our own court. And we were lucky to win the Tech game."

Soapy shrugged it off. "We didn't have Phillips in either of those games." He snapped the fingers of his right hand four times. "Mark my words, Chip. We'll take Eastern, Carlton, Midwestern, and Poly Tech just like that—one, two, three, four! By the way," he said, peering closely at Chip, "how do you feel?"

"Good."

"You don't look so good. Stone ought to let you off for three or four days."

"I don't *want* off. Besides, there's nothing due next week, and I can get to bed earlier."

"From what I hear, Chip, you'd *better* rest up."

"What do you mean?"

"Well, Murph Kelly has been hinting around about you needin' a rest."

"You're kidding, right, Soapy?"

"No, I'm not."

Chip said nothing more, but he was doing a lot of thinking. Kelly *had* been checking him out more closely than usual. The thing to do, he reflected, was to give the trainer plenty of room.

The weather changed Saturday morning. The sky was overcast and gloomy, and it was much warmer, even humid. It remained that way all day, and by early evening the streets and walks were filled with slush and water. Chip and Soapy tramped through the wet streets to Assembly Hall along with a small group of fans.

Chip dressed quickly and pretended to be full of energy to conceal his lethargy from Murph Kelly, but it wasn't easy. He had no desire to play basketball that night, and he wished the game were over. During the warm-up drills he felt cold and kept his jacket on until the game started.

Soapy had been right about Eastern. It was an easy game. Eastern had ranked at the bottom of the conference standings before the game and was still there when it was over. Stone used everyone on the squad, and Chip spent a lot of time on the bench.

It was the first time Stone had ever given Soapy much of a chance to play, and Chip noticed the coach watched his pal closely.

Soapy could thread a needle with the ball when it came to passing, and he was a deadeye shot—especially from the outside. But Stone's style of play practically eliminated his favorite shots, and Soapy had no chance to display his three-point expertise. Everyone played and everyone scored, and State coasted to a 90-67 win.

After the game, Chip and Soapy dressed quickly, said good night, and walked swiftly up the players' ramp to the main entrance of Assembly Hall. The two friends walked across the parking lot where State University fans were still jockeying their cars for an exit. Red brake lights dotted the parking lot as cars nudged forward and stopped, nudged forward and stopped. Within ten minutes, Chip and Soapy were downtown.

With the exception of two bookstores, some restaurants, and a few fast-food franchises, most of the businesses downtown were closed. Only a few people were on the streets or in the stores. Grayson's was no different, and only a few customers came in during the rest of the evening. Soapy helped Chip and Mitzi close up, and then Mitzi insisted on driving them home.

When they reached Jeff, a bunch of the guys were lounging around talking in the first floor study room, and Soapy jumped right in. Chip thought it looked like fun, but he decided against joining the crowd and wearily climbed the stairs to room 212 and his bed.

As he climbed gratefully into bed, he realized he was exhausted. And, to make it worse, their next three ball games would all be real dog fights, right down to the final buzzer.

Carlton, a strong independent, had beaten State earlier in the season by two points on the Statesmen home court. Chip had scored forty-one points in that game, but he racked up only twenty-six in this one. Fortunately, two of his points came in the last second and enabled State to come from behind and win, 74-73. Stone used every player on the team, and the trip back to University was a happy one. The win brought their season record to twelve wins and four losses, and they were still 8-1 in the conference.

They were back on the road again on Friday and won another important conference game, beating Midwestern 73-68. That gave them nine conference victories with only one loss and an overall record of 13-4.

Saturday afternoon, Mrs. Grayson came down to the store and spent an hour visiting with Chip and the rest of the staff. She was excited about Mr. Grayson's steady improvement. Her happiness was so contagious that she raised the morale of everyone in the store.

Chip's spirits were high after Mrs. Grayson's visit, and he felt almost like his old self. The feeling carried him through the first half of the Poly Tech game that night, but in the second half all his strength seemed to flow out of him. Stone recognized his condition and sent Speed in to replace him.

Speed was fast and a good shot, but he lacked Chip's playmaking abilities, and the Statesmen's attack faltered. Poly Tech quickly took advantage of the lapse and spurted into the lead. Stone had no alternative but to send Chip back in. He called on all his fight and determination, and his leadership lifted his teammates, gave them encouragement, and helped them pull themselves together. They fought back and went two points ahead with ten seconds to play. Chip led them into Stone's stall then, and they managed to hold onto the ball and last it out to win by two points, 78-76.

After the game, Soapy and Speed went back to the store to help Chip close up before returning to Jeff. He was still tired, but Chip's spirits were high. State had won eight straight games under Stone and stood 9-1 in the conference, with only seven more league games to play. *We can do it!* he exulted.

But on Sunday morning, Chip woke up with a raging headache.

Every muscle and joint in his body ached, and he felt sluggish, sleepy, and shivery all over. Soapy had made his bed and gone for breakfast and the papers, so Chip decided to rest a little longer.

A few minutes later, the redhead barged noisily through the door as usual, puffing and blowing. He stopped short when he saw Chip still in bed. "Hey! What's with you?"

"Nothing. Just sleeping in."

"Oh, yeah," Soapy said speculatively. "Who are you kidding? You're coming down with something."

"Sure. Laziness."

"You have a fever?"

"I don't know. Maybe. I feel like I'm catching a cold. Anyway, I'm still sleepy."

"That's good! You sleep. I'll see you after church."

"You've got two hours before it's time to go to church."

"I know, I know," Soapy said impatiently. "You feel like reading the papers? No, I guess not. Hold it a sec. I'll give you a Soapy Smith sports capsule.

"First, Kinser is still leading the scoring race with a 41.4 average. You're second with 36.7, and Henninger is third with 35.9.

"Next! A & M is still undefeated and leads the conference twelve to zip; Northern State is second with ten and zero, and good ole State is third with a record of nine and one."

Soapy stopped and squared his jaw. "You know something, Chip? It just doesn't seem right for coaches like Brannon to win *all* the time."

"He doesn't win all the time."

"Sure seems like it," Soapy said glumly. "Well, Southwestern is setting the pace on the national scene with sixteen consecutive wins. Wilson University and Northern State are tied for the runner-up spot with identical records: sixteen wins and one loss each.

"Our A & M friends are fourth with fifteen and one, and Templeton is in fifth place with a record of fifteen and two. Enough! I'm outta here for awhile. See you later."

Chip dozed until nearly eleven o'clock and then forced himself to get up and shave. He started to dress but was suddenly dizzy and too tired to move. He thought about it for a minute or so and then piled back into bed, pulling his quilt up around his chin. Soapy was back an hour later with some medicine and a double chocolate milk shake. "Here," he said, "take this."

"What is it?"

"Some cold medicine Murph Kelly gave me."

"Where did you see him?"

"At the gym."

"On Sunday?"

"Yep. Di Santis and Slater were there too."

"What were *they* doing there?"

"Murph was working on Dom's knee."

"What was wrong with Slater?"

"Nothing. He was waiting for Dom. They had an appointment with the coach; at least, that's what they said."

"What about?"

"Come on, Chip, how do I know?"

Chip studied his pal's eyes for a second. The redhead was a great actor, but Chip knew all of his tricks. "Come off it, Soapy," he said. "Quit stalling. What were Dom and Rudy going to see the coach about?"

"About, well, about the team."

"What about the team? *I'm* the captain. Why didn't I hear about it?"

"There's a lot of things you haven't heard," Soapy said mysteriously.

"For instance?" Chip prodded.

"Well, the guys think you ought to have time off from practice."

"What guys?"

"Oh, Dom and Rudy, and, well, all of them. They think Stone ought to give you more of a break."

"He *is* giving me a break, Soapy. What about late curfew?"

"It isn't enough."

"Wouldn't that be *my* problem?"

"Wait a sec, Chip. You're no superman. You've got to admit that having the chance to study three or four afternoons a week would mean that you could go to bed at a decent hour instead of studying all night. You can't sit there and tell me more time off wouldn't help."

"Sure it would help . . . a lot. But it wouldn't be fair to the rest of the team, *nor* to Coach Stone. I wouldn't think of it."

"Everyone else is on scholarship."

"You're not."

"No, but I'm not running a store, and I'm getting a lot of rest on the bench. You're working your head off in school and at the store and in the games. There's a difference."

"Not much."

"Dom and Rudy think there is. Anyway—"

"Go on," Chip urged.

"Well, anyway, they went to talk to Stone and—"

"About me? About more time off for me?"

"So they said."

"Fine friend *you* are!" Chip said shortly, throwing back his quilt and leaping out of bed. "I'll settle this right now!"

CHAPTER 12

Ex-Athletics List

SOAPY SMITH sank wearily down on his bed and watched Chip yank his clothes out of the closet. "What are you going to do?" he asked.

"I'm going to find Dom and Rudy and tell them to stay away from Coach Stone and to mind their own business. Then I'm going to tell them what I think of them. That's what I'm going to do!"

Soapy threw his hands up in the air in a gesture of despair. "No, Chip," he moaned. "You can't do that!"

"Can't I? Wait and see!"

"But they didn't want you to know anything about it. Besides, it's too late. They've already talked to the coach."

"For goodness' sake," Chip said irritably. "Now what am I going to do?"

"Forget about it," Soapy said. "Go back to bed. I'll call Mitzi and get her to open the store."

"Nothing doing. That's *my* job."

"Listen, Chip," Soapy pleaded, "you shouldn't go out feeling the way you do. There's never that much business on

Sundays. It's no problem. Mitzi would come right down. You know that. Besides, you just took some medicine. C'mon, Chip. Use your head."

"You should have stopped it," Chip said over his shoulder. "What will the coach think?"

"I don't know, Chip."

"Why didn't Dom and Rudy say something to me?"

"Man, Chip, how could they? They knew you wouldn't stand for it. Listen to yourself right now."

Soapy's voice was conciliatory, but it grew serious and more forceful as he continued. "Listen, Chip, your health is important to the guys. What happens if you get sick? What if you get so sick you can't even go to school or take care of the store?"

"I'm not going to get sick. Now that those major assignments are over for awhile, I can take it a little easier. If only the guys hadn't gone to see the coach! Why didn't you stop them?"

"How could I?"

"Then why did you tell me?"

"I didn't *mean* to tell you. Man, Chip! They'll never speak to me again if they find out I told you. If you say anything, I'll be in an *awful* spot."

Chip was thinking that Soapy was probably right. Dom and Rudy would be angry with Soapy. And if he was going to be fair about it, his constant probing had practically forced Soapy to tell him about the meeting. Well, it was a cinch to decide; he wasn't going to put his best friend in that kind of position.

"All right!" he said decisively. "Have it your way. I won't say anything. Let's forget it. I just hope the coach doesn't think I sent them."

"Come on, Chip. He knows you better than that."

Despite Soapy's protests, Chip was determined to go to Grayson's. Soapy waited at the door while Chip made a tour of the store. By the time he had finished up his responsibilities, Cara Davis, Lonnie Freeman, and Kurt Welch had reported in and Soapy was busy at the fountain.

It was a cold, windy afternoon and evening, and few people were on the streets. Chip made a tour around eight o'clock and found only two or three customers at the counters, so he went back upstairs and called Mrs. Grayson to suggest they close the store early. She agreed and told him to close up right away and send the staff home. Mrs. Grayson's voice sounded more cheerful than it had in the last week as she told Chip she had just talked to Mr. Grayson. "The doctor said he can come home in another ten days or so."

"Did he ask about the basketball team?"

"Yes, he did. The doctor wants him to fully rest, so he won't let him read the papers or watch TV. But I've been keeping him up to date on all the games and about your scoring. Now you close up and go on home."

Chip went back downstairs and told Soapy to pass the word that Mrs. Grayson said everyone could go home. In a few minutes everything was in order. He turned out the lights and started up Main Street with Soapy. When they reached the State Theater, they stopped to look at the movie posters.

"Let's go in," Soapy suggested. "This is the last night we'll have a chance to relax for a whole month."

"How do you figure that?"

"Our last game is on the fourth of March. That's exactly a month from last night," Soapy said.

"How about the NCAA Tournament and March Madness?"

"That's extra. That's rich chocolate frosting on a double chocolate cake. And we're gonna lick it clear off after we lick A & M and Northern State."

"I hope you're right. Anyway, I think I'll pass on the movie and go on back to the dorm and catch up on my reading."

"Mind if I catch the movie?" Soapy asked.

"Of course not."

The redhead ducked quickly into the theater entrance, and Chip yanked his coat up around his neck and leaned into the wind. Fifteen minutes later Chip was home at Jeff and in his room. He read for a while and then went to bed, falling asleep long before Soapy got home from the movies.

Monday morning Chip followed his usual routine. He opened up Grayson's, hustled back to campus for his first class, returned to the store around lunchtime, returned to school for more classes, and then hustled over to Assembly Hall for practice.

Murph Kelly called to him as soon as he entered the locker room. "Doc Terring wants to see you. Right away."

"What for?"

"A checkup."

"Now wait a minute, Murph. I'm all right."

"*I* didn't turn you in."

"Then how do you know he wants to give me a checkup?"

"Because he said so."

"That's funny," Chip said slowly. "Someone had to tell him."

Chip turned and walked slowly out of the locker room and up the stairs to the second floor where Dr. Mike Terring, State University's Athletic Department physician, kept an office when he wasn't up at the medical center. The physician's assistant, Sondra Ruiz, glanced up when Chip entered. "Hi, Chip!" she smiled in greeting.

"Hi," Chip said.

"Dr. Terring is expecting you," she said, gesturing to the office directly behind her. "Go right on in."

Dr. Terring was sitting at his desk reading when Chip entered. The tall, friendly man looked up, quickly rose, and walked around his desk to extend his hand in a warm handshake. "Glad to see you, Chip," he said. "It's about time you paid me a visit."

"What for, Doc?" Chip asked anxiously. "There isn't anything wrong with me."

"That isn't what I hear," Terring said. "S'pose you come in here and let me find out."

Chip followed Terring into the adjoining room and looked around. It contained only the barest essentials of an examination room—a small desk, a table, wall charts, scales, cabinets, and two chairs.

"This is foolish," Chip protested.

"Take off your shirt," Terring said brusquely.

"Who said there was something wrong with me?" Chip demanded.

"Oh, a number of people," Terring said pleasantly.

"You mean you won't tell."

"Perhaps. By the way, I've been watching you in the games, and you haven't looked up to par. Now please stop your yacking and sit down and relax."

It was a thorough examination. Terring weighed him, checked his blood pressure, took his temperature, peered into his ears and down his throat, probed his neck glands, listened to his chest with a stethoscope, and finally made him do a standing run for a full minute and then checked him again. Then he told Chip to put his shirt on and led the way back into his office. On the way he asked his assistant to pull Chip's physical card out of the file. He motioned the anxious player to a chair and, sitting down behind his desk, made several notations on a pad.

Sondra Ruiz entered with the card, and Terring asked her to phone Murph Kelly. "Tell Murph I'd like him to come on up." Then he compared Chip's card with the notes he had made on his desk pad. "Well, Chip," he said reluctantly, "it's bad news. I have to put you on the ex-athletics list."

"No!" Chip protested, leaping to his feet. *"No! Nothing doing!"* He strode nervously back and forth across the office.

"Sorry, Chip, I have no alternative."

"But there's nothing wrong with me."

"Now wait a second," Terring said sternly. "You sit down, young man." He motioned to a chair and waited until Chip was seated before continuing.

"There are a *number* of things wrong with you. First, you have a temperature. You're suffering from the flu, and you're clearly stressed out. That little demonstration you just put on proves the point. That outburst was completely out of character for you. Further, you've lost eight pounds."

"Everyone trains down during the season," Chip protested.

"That hasn't been my experience," Terring said decisively. "Your normal weight during the season is one-ninety, and you know it."

"I've been working hard, that's all."

"That isn't 'all.' You're rapidly approaching a state of anemia."

"Anemia! With my appetite?"

"That's right."

"Now wait a minute, Doc. How long is this ex-athletic thing going to last? All the important games are coming up, and I've got to play."

"I know," Terring said. "I have a schedule right here on my desk."

"How many games will I miss?"

"That depends upon how quickly you recuperate."

"But you didn't say how long."

Voices interrupted them, and Sondra Ruiz escorted Murph Kelly into the office and then returned to her desk. "Hello, Murph," Terring said. "I guess you know why we're here."

"Yes, Doc," Kelly said, glancing at Chip, "I do."

"Chip needs a good rest and he needs to put on some weight," Terring said. "Here are a couple of prescriptions and—well, I'll leave the rest to you."

Kelly took the prescriptions and looked expectantly at Terring. "How long?"

"Two, maybe three weeks—"

Chip felt a quiet, choking surge of anger build up inside him. He could hardly breathe. "No!" he said slowly and vehemently. "I can't miss three weeks. I have some rights."

"And I have my duty as the team physician," Terring said softly.

Chip got up, walked around behind Terring's desk and checked the schedule under the glass desktop. Murph Kelly followed, and the three of them scanned the list of games.

Wed.	Feb. 8	*CATHEDRAL	AWAY
Fri.	Feb. 10	*SOUTHERN	HOME
Wed.	Feb. 15	WILSON TECH	AWAY
Fri.	Feb. 17	TEMPLETON	HOME
Sat.	Feb. 18	*A & M	HOME
Wed.	Feb. 22	*WESTERN	AWAY
Sat.	Feb. 25	*NORTHERN STATE	AWAY
Wed.	Mar. 1	SOUTHWESTERN	AWAY
Fri.	Mar. 3	*A & M	AWAY
Sat.	Mar. 4	*NORTHERN STATE	HOME

Chip counted the games and then glanced at the desk calendar. "This is the sixth," he fretted. "Three weeks would be up to the twenty-seventh, and I would miss the next seven games. Five of those are in the conference: Cathedral, Southern, A & M, Western, and Northern State. Even if it was only two weeks, I'd miss three conference games."

Chip faced Terring and shook his head stubbornly. "I won't let you do it, Doc. You can't do this to me. To the team. We've got a *great* team, and it isn't fair. We can win the conference! Maybe the national championship!"

He walked around the desk and slumped down in his chair, dismayed and sick at heart.

There was a long, heavy silence. Then Kelly walked over and placed a hand on Chip's shoulder. "Listen, Chipper," he said softly, "basketball is a big thing with you right now. But your health is a bigger thing. Doc thinks a lot of you. We all do. I'm speaking for the team as well as for myself. We would rather lose all the games, even cancel the schedule, than jeopardize your health."

"But three weeks," Chip said dejectedly.

"Perhaps it won't be three weeks," Terring said gently. "Perhaps you will make a comeback faster than I think. Why not give it a good try? You go along now and follow Kelly's suggestions and take your medicine and get your rest. And another thing: I want you to forget all about basketball. No watching practices and no games.

"Now suppose you come back to see me next Monday. We'll see how much progress you've made. All right?"

Chip nodded and slowly hauled himself to his feet. He realized he'd been out of line, and this was not the time to argue. Doc Terring knew what he was doing, and Chip wasn't going to change his mind. Chagrined, Chip also realized he had been wrong to take his frustration out on Doc.

Chip straightened his shoulders and quietly extended his hand. "Dr. Terring, I'm sorry for acting the way I did and for the things I said to you. Please accept my apology."

Doc Terring met Chip's steady gaze and firmly clasped his hand. "Of course, Chip. You just get better. That's all any of us want."

Chip, relieved, nodded his thanks and headed out the door.

Soapy had the right idea. The practice time could be used to rest. Maybe he would be all right in a week. It was time to start taking care of himself, he reflected. First, though, he had to let Mrs. Grayson know all about this ex-athletics nonsense before it hit the papers.

CHAPTER 13

The Soapy Smith Health Plan

MITZI SAVRILL stopped her work on the computer and looked up in surprise when Chip entered the office. She didn't speak. The expression on Chip's face stopped her cheery "Hello," and she watched him curiously as he walked over to the desk and dropped heavily into the chair behind George Grayson's desk.

"What's the matter?" she asked gently when he was seated. "Don't you feel well?"

Chip leaned back in the chair and ignored the question. Abruptly, he swiveled the chair to face Mitzi directly. "How do I look?" he countered.

Mitzi studied him a moment before replying. "Well," she said in a matter-of-fact voice, "you look tired and discouraged and half-sick. What's wrong?"

"Doc Terring benched me."

Mitzi gasped in dismay. "No wonder you look sick," she managed. "What's the trouble?"

"I'm anemic, or so he says. And according to him, I'm eight pounds underweight."

"You don't have to go to the hospital or anything like that, do you?"

"No, I can work and go to school, but he won't let me play basketball."

Mitzi whistled softly. "That's big trouble for the team," she said in a concerned voice.

"They'll get along," Chip said quickly. And then, reddening just a bit, Chip added quietly, "Thanks for listening, Mitzi. You're a good friend to Soapy and me." He swiveled the chair back around and expelled a deep breath. "Well, I better get this over with. I have to call Mrs. Grayson."

Chip called her and explained about Dr. Terring's decision and, before she had a chance to think much about it, told her that there was nothing seriously wrong. "I've just been studying too much," he explained.

Mrs. Grayson didn't panic, but she did ask a lot of questions, and Chip could tell she wasn't fully satisfied. Before ending the conversation, she said, "I'll be in to see you tomorrow afternoon. What would be the best time?"

Chip told her 2:30 would be fine and breathed a deep sigh of relief when she hung up. That was the beginning of a hectic evening. Bill Bell, sports editor of the *Herald,* called him on the phone to check the story, and he had no more than finished talking to him when Cara Davis buzzed the intercom to say that Jim Locke of the *News* was on his way up to the office.

Locke spent half an hour with him and left after stating that he had to put the story on the AP wire. Chip was glad he had talked to the *News* sports editor himself because Locke frequently jumped to conclusions in his stories. He was particularly adept at suggestive phrasing and exaggeration.

Around nine o'clock, Dom Di Santis and Rudy Slater shuffled into the storeroom looking for Chip. They were worried about their teammate. Coach Stone had gotten the bad news from Murph Kelly and announced Chip's absence to the entire squad at practice that afternoon. Chip noticed the bitterness in their voices when they mentioned Stone's name, but he let it pass.

Soapy dropped in before leaving a little before ten o'clock to report the reaction of the fans and to find out if there was anything he could do before going home.

"Seems like every basketball fan in the state has been in to find out what it's all about," he said.

Chip sent the redhead on his way after promising to come directly home to Jeff.

He and Mitzi closed up half an hour later, and Mitzi drove him back to the dorm. Chip thanked his friend and moved slowly and dejectedly up the walk to the front porch stairs, and then on up the steps to the second floor. For the first time, he let his thoughts run their bitter course. With the important conference games coming up and his teammates feeling as they did about Stone, it could very well mean the collapse of State's championship dreams. "Nothing doing," he muttered. "I can't let this happen. They've got to keep going."

He had reached his room now, and he could see Soapy hunting and pecking away with his two index fingers at his computer keyboard. Chip opened the door wider and stopped in surprise. Speed, Biggie, Red, and Fireball were sprawled all over the place—on the beds, on Soapy's battered, overstuffed chair from home, and on the floor. Standing in the doorway, Chip surveyed the room. "What's going on?" he demanded.

The redhead looked up and then tapped his watch. "You're not on schedule," he growled.

"On schedule? What do you mean?"

"I mean, well, you might as well know now as later. We had a board meeting."

"What about?"

"Well," Soapy explained, "Speed, Biggie, Red, Fireball, and me, er, I, have decided to help you out a bit at the store and with your studying and—" He paused and accentuated the words, "to supervise your program."

"What program?"

"Your daily program," Red said.

"What sort of nonsense is this?"

"It isn't nonsense, Chip," Fireball said earnestly. "We've got to get you back on your feet and back on the team."

Chip snorted. "*On my feet!* You talk as if I were sick in bed. This is all a lot of nonsense."

"Murph Kelly and Doc Terring obviously don't think so," Soapy reminded him. He turned back to the computer. "Wait until I finish this."

Chip closed the door and then climbed over Speed to get to the closet to hang up his jacket. While he was removing his wet shoes, he thought about his friends. He knew them well; he knew their personalities, their moods, and their fun-loving natures. Now their faces were serious and the usual bantering and laughter were missing.

Their "board" meetings had been this way for a long time. The meetings had started out in fun when the Valley Falls crowd first arrived on the State campus. It was really just an extension of the Hilton Athletic Club. That's what they had called Chip's backyard in Valley Falls. There they had gathered to practice the sports they loved and to talk about dreams, problems, and the everyday trials of growing up.

Once they had arrived at State, these same friends had made a point of getting together at frequent intervals to talk about home and their problems as freshmen. At that time they were enjoying the thrill of freedom from home and the responsibilities a college freshman faces for the first time.

The meetings had helped overcome homesickness, although none of them would have admitted it. It wasn't long until they began to realize that the meetings represented a simple fraternity. They were bonded together in college as they had been in high school in Valley Falls. It was a peculiar sort of association; there were no vows, dues, officers, or formalities. There was but one purpose—friendship. The board meetings had continued through their freshman and sophomore years, and they were still at it now as juniors.

THE SOAPY SMITH HEALTH PLAN

There had been just the five Valley Falls pals at first: Soapy, Speed, Biggie, Red, and Chip Then Fireball Finley had appeared on the scene on a State football scholarship. The burly fullback liked the Valley Falls group, and they liked him. He had been one of them ever since.

Board meetings had nothing to do with the extemporaneous gatherings when they got together to discuss sports, campus activities, or studies. When a board meeting was called, it meant that someone needed help. The person didn't necessarily have to be a member of their group; it could be someone they liked or thought deserving of their assistance.

Chip had changed into sweats by this time. He walked over and sat down beside Fireball just as Soapy finished printing copies for everyone. With a dramatic flourish, the redhead lifted the pages out of the printer tray and nodded with satisfaction. He handed the sheets around the room, presenting Chip's last.

"There!" Soapy said smugly. "Here's your copy of the Soapy Smith Health plan."

THE SOAPY SMITH HEALTH PLAN

7:30 A.M.	Medicine and Juices
8:00 A.M.	Breakfast (Grayson's)
10:30 A.M.	Morning Snack (student union)
1:00 P.M.	Lunch (Grayson's)
3:00 P.M.	Rest and Study (Jeff)
4:00 P.M.	Warm Milk and Hot Tea and Honey (Jeff)
5:45 P.M.	Leave for Work
6:45 P.M.	Rest (Mr. Grayson's office)
7:15 P.M.	Dinner (Grayson's)
8:00 P.M.	Work and Study
9:00 P.M.	Milk Shake a la Smith
10:30 P.M.	Close Store
11:00 P.M.	Bedtime Stew and Medicine (Jeff)
11:15 P.M.	Bed: Lights Out!

Chip read the schedule and then looked up and grinned. "What makes you think I can follow this? What about my classes?"

Soapy served as secretary of the board meetings and was always the spokesman. "You go to all of them, of course," he said. "The schedule isn't perfect, but it's a general outline. And," he added grimly, "we're going to see that you follow it."

"Who dreamed all of this up?" Chip demanded.

"Murph Kelly," Soapy said indignantly. "Are you going to cooperate or not?"

"He'll cooperate," Biggie growled, curling up his forearm to show his biceps. Despite his intimidating appearance, Biggie's brawn encased a gentle spirit and one of the kindest hearts Chip had ever known.

Laughing, Chip sized up Biggie's 240-pound frame and the bulging muscles and nodded in agreement. "You win, Biggie!" he said, grinning. "I know when I'm well off."

"Good," Soapy said. "Now I've got to prepare your bedtime stew."

"Bedtime *stew!*" Chip echoed. "Oh, no!" he gasped, laughing and rolling back on the bed. "This is too much. *Bedtime stew!*"

All of the guys—with the exception of Soapy—joined in Chip's laughter. Soapy simply ignored them. The others watched patiently as Soapy made a big production of lifting a small microwave out of a box from the closet and plugging it into the outlet.

"Man, you got a microwave?" Speed exclaimed.

"It's Mitzi's. She lent it to me for the duration," Soapy explained. Reaching to the shelf above his desk, Soapy pulled down a small can, a can opener, a saltshaker, two spoons, a large soup bowl, and a box of crackers. Then he opened the window and removed a small carton of milk and a single stick of butter from the ledge. After pouring the milk into the large bowl, he placed it in the microwave and twirled the timer.

Next he held up the small can. "Oysters," he said brightly.

Then he tossed the can to Speed. "Speedy," he said, "open 'em up and pour off the water. I've got to warm this milk to exactly the right temperature. Ahem!"

"Right temperature?" Speed said sarcastically. "What are you going to use for a thermometer?"

"His elbow!" Fireball shouted.

That set off another shout of laughter. Soapy held up his hands and pleaded for silence. "Hold it, guys," he said. "*Please!* I've gotta think!"

"Oh, no!" Speed said, rolling his eyes upward. "Oh, no! He's gotta think!"

The guys laughed again, but Soapy went on ignoring them. He took the can of oysters from Speed, removed the bowl of hot milk from the microwave, and ceremoniously dumped the oysters into the milk. "This has to come to an exact boil," he said, adding a pat of butter and some salt and returning the bowl to the microwave. Two minutes later, the bell dinged, and Soapy removed the steaming broth. "All right, Chipper," he said proudly. "It's all yours."

"Play along with him, Chip," Speed advised. "I'll call his psychiatrist."

Chip sat down at the desk and tried the stew. It was excellent. "This is good!" he said in surprise.

"This kind of cooperation I like," Soapy said happily.

"It actually smells good," Biggie observed.

"You mean great," Soapy corrected. He turned to Speed. "All right, Speedy, s'pose you wipe out the microwave."

Speed groaned, but he took the sponge Soapy offered him and went to work. Soapy got two thumbtacks out of the desk and picked up three of the schedules. "Now, Chip," he said briskly, "one of these goes under the glass on Mr. Grayson's desk, one goes behind the cash register on the fountain, and the other one stays here on your bulletin board. OK?"

"OK," Chip repeated, grinning.

"I must advise you," Soapy continued, "that the health plan is to be observed religiously. Oh, I meant to ask you. What did Mrs. Grayson say?"

"What do you mean?"

Soapy shrugged his shoulders and spread his hands. "It's obvious, Dr. Watson, obvious. You had to tell her before it hit the papers."

Chip nodded. "That's right, and I did. She seemed a little upset. Anyway, she's coming down to the store tomorrow afternoon."

"What about Mr. Grayson?" Fireball asked.

"Mrs. Grayson said his doctor isn't allowing him to read the papers."

"That's a break," Speed said fervently.

"All right, all right!" Soapy scolded. "It's long past my patient's bedtime. Oh! Guys, before you go, er, well, unaccustomed as I am to talking—"

"Oh, man!" Speed moaned.

"I mean public speaking," Soapy continued, with a threatening glare at Speed, "I want to take this opportunity to thank all of you for your cooperation. Especially you, Mr. Morris. I never—"

Soapy was snowed under by a flurry of pillows and gales of laughter.

"Hold it down, guys!" Biggie warned. "It's late and Chipper needs his beauty rest."

That quieted the guys, and they whispered good night and walked quietly to their rooms. Soapy closed the door, and within fifteen minutes he and Chip were asleep.

CHAPTER 14

A Disastrous Nose Dive

TUESDAY MORNING, before he went to school, Soapy stuck around to see that Chip got off on the right foot with the health program. And when Chip reached Grayson's to open up, Fireball was already there. He made sure Chip got his breakfast and then accompanied him to the campus where they separated to go to their nine o'clock classes.

Biggie picked him up outside the Metcalf Science Building at ten o'clock and walked along with him to the student union for some warm milk and chocolate chip cookies. The big guy merely smiled when Chip protested that he didn't like warm milk. Chip shrugged and drank it down.

After his eleven o'clock class, Chip started for Grayson's. On the way, he passed a newsstand, which reminded him that the story was undoubtedly in the papers. But he had no desire to read about it and continued on to work.

He checked the mail and was on his way down the steps from the office when he saw Speed. "What are you doing down here?" he asked.

"You know why I'm here," Speed retorted. "It's my job to see that you have your lunch."

Philip "Whitty" Whittemore had evidently been alerted, because he came along at that precise moment with a tray of food. "Come on now, Chip," he said, starting up the steps to the office. "Get it while it's hot."

Chip turned and followed Whitty to the office. Speed was right behind him. Whittemore arranged Chip's lunch on the desk and headed back to the fountain. Speed sat down in a chair and pulled a newspaper out of his backpack. "The story is spread all over the sports pages," he said. "Have you seen it?"

Chip shook his head. "No, Speed, and I don't want to."

"It lists all the games you've played in and the points you've scored," Speed ventured. "It says this is quite a blow to State's basketball hopes."

"I don't know about that," Chip said, "but it sure knocked me into the bleachers."

"That goes for all of us," Speed said gloomily.

Chip took in Speed's downcast face and grinned. "What are you trying to do," he said lightly, "cheer me up?"

He waited until Speed smiled and continued quickly, "With all the attention I'm getting from you and Soapy and the rest of the guys, I'll be back before the week is out."

"Man, you haven't seen anything yet," his friend said brightly, rising from his chair. "Well, I've got to get back to campus." Just as he was about to go out the door, Speed turned, winked, pointed at his friend, and said, "You finish eating! See you tonight."

Mrs. Grayson arrived at exactly 2:30, agitated and worried. But the lines in her forehead relaxed after Chip explained that Dr. Terring had said he was to come back the following Monday. She left after reporting that Mr. Grayson would soon be home.

Fireball showed up at three o'clock to accompany Chip on his way home to Jeff for rest and study. Chip grumbled a bit, but he took off. When he got back to his room, Biggie was there, grinning widely and holding a mug of warm milk.

Chip studied awhile, took a nap, and then started back to work. It was a pleasant walk until he reached Main Street. Then it seemed that he met someone every step of the way who knew about his bad luck. Many of the fans were mere acquaintances; some he didn't know at all. He was courteous to everybody, but he didn't stop to talk; he just kept moving.

"Tough luck, Chip."

"How long are you out for, Chipper?"

"Better get well quick, Hilton. The team needs you."

"How are you feeling?"

"Jim Locke said you might be out for the season. Any truth in it?"

That one nearly floored Chip, but he came right back. "No, *way!*" he said quickly. "I'll be back in a week."

He spent as much time as possible in the office the rest of the day in an attempt to avoid any more fans. Soapy brought him a double chocolate milk shake around nine o'clock and visited with him while he drank it.

"We had a lousy practice," Soapy said in disgust, looking down at his shoes.

"What was wrong?"

"Everything! And I do mean *everything*. The guys were all feeling beat and Stone was kind of edgy."

"What do you mean, 'edgy'?"

"Aw, you know how he gets—cranky and irritable. Anyway, he was trying to develop another combination, and every guy he put in your place flopped; and it was, well, a wasted afternoon."

"You can't call it wasted, Soapy. He has to get the team ready for Cathedral."

"Anyone can take Cathedral."

"We didn't take them. They beat us by fifteen points," Chip reminded him.

Soapy nodded his agreement. "Sure! But then you weren't playing and we didn't have Speed or Phillips either."

"Nor Soapy Smith," Chip added.

"I didn't play then, and I'm not playing now," Soapy said bitterly. "I'm just wasting a lot of time for nothing."

"You don't mean that, Soapy," Chip said gently. "How would you get rid of all the excess energy you build up?"

Soapy snorted in disgust. "I sure don't get rid of any energy sitting on the bench."

"How about the practices?"

"They're all right, I guess," Soapy admitted grudgingly, "but a guy likes to play in the games." He picked up the milk shake glass, hesitated a moment, and then changed the subject. "This health plan might seem a little silly, Chip, but we're all getting a big kick out of it."

Chip got to his feet and punched Soapy playfully on the chin. "I know, Soapy," he said. "I think it's great. It's sure making things a lot easier for me. See you in a couple of hours. Oyster stew again tonight?"

Soapy straightened up and expanded his chest. "I'm sorry, Mr. Hilton," he said coldly, "that's a top-shelf secret." Then, clipping his words short and speaking rapidly, he continued, "Much of the value of our health menus depends upon the element of surprise we inject—"

"Stop!" Chip cried, holding up both of his hands. "You win."

Soapy pivoted and walked stiffly to the door. Then he bowed and clattered down the steps. After the redhead left, Chip sat at the desk a long time thinking about his best pal. Despite the act he had just put on, Soapy was about as low in spirits as it was possible for him to get, and Chip didn't like it. Not one bit.

He got up and paced back and forth across the office. Stone had never given Soapy a real chance. It was the same old story, he reflected; you can never tell a book by its cover. Soapy looked more like a football player than a basketball player, but he was both. As far as that was concerned, Chip was thinking, Soapy was the best man on the squad to take his place as a playmaker. And, he added to himself, if he ever got the chance, he would tell Coach Stone just that.

He kept busy the rest of the evening, but right before closing time he got to thinking about Soapy and the guys. There was too much consistency in his friends' methods to account for chance meetings. He decided to ask Fireball about it and strolled up to the end of the fountain. He caught Finley's eye, and the big athlete walked up and leaned on the counter with his elbow. "Warm milk?" he asked.

"Nothing doing," Chip retorted sweetly, "all I want is some information."

"Be my guest," Fireball said.

"All right. How come it just so happened you were here this morning and again this afternoon? What about your classes?"

Fireball laughed. "That's easy, buddy. We had a look at our class schedules for every day in the week and made sure one of us could be on hand to check your progress on the health plan."

"You're kidding."

"Not a chance. Have a look." Fireball pulled his class schedule and a copy of Soapy's health plan out of his pocket and laid them side by side on the counter. It required only a quick glance for Chip to check them.

"Satisfied?" Fireball asked.

Chip nodded. "I'm satisfied."

"All right, then," Fireball said, feigning belligerence, "you hit the road after you close up and don't stop until you get to Jeff. Let's see, according to the health plan, Soapy will have your bedtime snack ready at precisely eleven o'clock. It's now 10:30. That gives you half an hour to close up and get home. So don't fool around. Understand?"

Chip came to attention and gave Fireball a snappy salute. "Yes, sir," he said sharply.

Wednesday night, Chip got to thinking about the Cathedral game and found it impossible to concentrate on anything. He wandered aimlessly about the store, imagining Assembly Hall, the fans, the cheerleaders, and his teammates. He was living the game almost as vividly as if he were there.

Every game was vital now if the dream he had carried in his heart ever since the tournament in New York was to come true. He could still hear Coach Corrigan telling them good-bye after they beat Wilson University in the consolation game: *Come next March, you men will have taught Northern State a lesson in sportsmanship and good basketball and will have beaten Southwestern, and Chip will be the nation's top scorer and captain of the national champions. . . .*

In the stockroom, Lonnie Freeman and Skip Miller were listening to the game on a local University radio station, and Skip was keeping Chip posted on the score. It had been close all the way through, and Chip thought the second half would never end. At work in Mr. Grayson's office, he waited anxiously for the final score.

He heard Skip taking the steps two at a time and he sensed that State had won before the teenager even said a word. Skip burst through the doorway, gasping in relief. "They won, Chip, 66-64. It's only two points, but that's enough! They won!"

With the result of that game out of the way, Chip went back to work with a much higher degree of concentration. Later, on the way home, Soapy filled him in on the game details. "It was tight, Chipper. The guys played as if they had never seen one another before. Stone tried everyone on the squad in your place."

"Did you play?"

"About two minutes," Soapy said wryly.

Everyone was waiting in the first floor study room when they came home to Jeff. Speed was already there, talking about the game, and the guys called to Chip and Soapy to join them. But the redhead marched Chip past them and right up the stairs. After he had prepared the stew—beef and potatoes this time—he ordered Chip to bed, turned out the light, and went downstairs to tell the guys about his part in the victory.

Chip was beginning to feel rested, and it was hard to sleep. He lay there a long while thinking about the team and the conference and the tournament before he finally drifted off to sleep.

Coach Stone called him Thursday evening and told him he was sorry to hear about Dr. Terring's decision, but that it was for the best. "I guess it isn't necessary to tell you how rough it's going to be without you," he added. "I just hope you can get back for the A & M game. Let me know if I can help you in any way."

Chip's former routine had been of his own choosing. Now it seemed that he was being watched and directed by Soapy, Speed, Biggie, Red, or Fireball everywhere he went. Each friend acted as if it were his particular responsibility to see that the health program was religiously followed. It was good fun, and he was making progress. But that was the only fun he was to have for some time.

The Statesmen lost four games in a row, and State's conference championship hopes went into a disastrous nose dive. The first loss was to Southern, 71-65, in Assembly Hall. A defeat is always tough to take, and always hurts, but a defeat at home really stings.

After the Southern loss, Soapy came down to the store and walked home with him, but he didn't talk much about the game. Chip probed just enough to learn that Soapy hadn't played at all, so he dropped the subject and went to bed.

Sunday, the redhead got the papers, but he still didn't talk about the game. Chip didn't know what to say about the game and skipped the sports pages. He went to church and from there headed to Grayson's. Later that afternoon Mrs. Grayson visited the store.

Chip told her how much better he felt and she reported that Mr. Grayson might be coming home in another week. Chip walked her across the street to her car and then went back to work.

Monday came at last. Chip fretted and fumed through his morning classes and was too nervous to finish his lunch. After his one o'clock class, he set out for Assembly Hall. Sondra Ruiz greeted him warmly and told him Dr. Terring was expecting him. She sent Chip directly into the office.

"You look better already," Terring commented. "Let's find out."

The examination was brief but thorough. At the end, Dr. Terring shook his head. "I'm sorry to disappoint you, Chip," he said gently. "However, I can't give you an OK."

"But, Doc!"

Terring nodded. "I know. But there's no use getting upset or trying to make me change my mind. I'm as disappointed as you are. After all, Chip, I'm an alum of State University, and I want the basketball team to win as badly as anyone. However, I can't get around the facts."

"But I—"

"Just a moment. Sure you've made progress. A lot! But right now you're at the point where you can go either way—ahead or back. A reverse would keep you out for the season. Another week will mean all the difference in the world. I'll say this—if you make as much progress by next Monday as you made this past week, I can safely give you an OK."

"But I'll miss three more games. Wilson University and Templeton aren't so important, but A & M is a must."

"Not with me, Chip. No game is important enough for me to take a chance with your health. Nope, you see me on Monday, February 20, at three o'clock and not before. And stay away from basketball, Chip."

Coach Stone called him late that evening and said he had talked to Dr. Terring and that it was important for Chip to stick to his schedule and his medicine. Just before ending the conversation, Stone said, "Don't worry about the Southern loss. We've still got a good chance. You just get well."

The Statesmen took to the road on Wednesday and absorbed a 92-69 loss at the hands of Wilson University. The licking was not entirely unexpected, since Wilson was one of the powerhouses of the country and had a long home-court winning streak going. However, the Statesmen had beaten Wilson U. in New York in the tournament, and this twenty-three-point defeat upset everyone.

Chip was the target of attention wherever he went during the next two days, both on campus and on the streets of University.

"Better hurry up, Hilton. Season's nearly over."

"What's wrong with you anyway?"

"State isn't going anywhere without you. Better get with it!"

"You look fine to me, Hilton. How come you aren't playing?"

The barbs hurt, but he took them in stride. He didn't read the papers, and Soapy wasn't talking about basketball, so he knew nothing about the trouble brewing between Coach Stone and the players until Friday night after Soapy had left for the game. He went to the stockroom to check an order and found Skip sitting at the desk staring moodily out the window.

"It can't be that bad," Chip said lightly.

"It is."

"Want to tell me about it?"

Skip thought it over for a second and then nodded vigorously. "I guess Soapy will be mad at me, but I think you ought to know what's going on."

"What do you mean?"

"I don't know anything for sure, but there's a lot of talk going around that some of the players are going to quit the team."

"Are you sure?"

"I'm not positive, Chip, but that's what I heard."

"Thanks, Skip," Chip said. "I'll keep it confidential."

Chip went up to the office to think about the news. None of the varsity players had been around to see him for several days, and that in itself was strange. He decided to ask Soapy about it point-blank after the game.

Chip and everyone else had counted on a victory over Templeton. State had defeated the Templars in the Holiday Invitational, and hopes had been high for an easy home victory. But the visitors outfought the home team and pinned a seven-point defeat on the Statesmen, 81-74. The only consolation Chip got was the fact that it was not a conference game.

Soapy's spirits and remarks after the game were bitter enough to warn Chip that a real breach had developed between his teammates and Stone. It seemed as if the situation had reached the point where something had to give. He had sat the bench all year, Soapy fumed. It had been bad enough to miss the first few games of the schedule because of reporting late following football, but to sit and sit game after game was too much.

"We're going to give it all we've got tomorrow night and then we'll see what we see," Soapy said bitterly.

"What do you mean?"

But Soapy had evidently said more than he intended, and he wasn't going to do any more talking. He lapsed into silence, and Chip let it pass. He would see Dom and Rudy on Sunday. He wasn't going to get them upset before the vital A & M game.

On the way to work Saturday morning, Soapy got two copies of the *News* and gave one to Chip. A little later in the morning, up in Mr. Grayson's office, Chip read Jim Locke's column and the other sports news. A & M was leading the league with a thirteen and one record; Northern State was in second place with eleven victories and two losses, and State was third with ten wins and two defeats.

Chip had a composite conference schedule, and he studied it carefully. In addition to tonight's game, State had one more game with A & M at Archton and two with Northern State. A & M and Northern State had their own headaches, since they had a two-game series to play against each other. A win for the Statesmen tonight would put them within striking distance of the leaders. He sure hoped he would be back in time to play against Northern State. He had a couple of scores to settle with the Northerners.

It was tough to wait; Chip's nerves were all out of whack, and he became more nervous with each passing hour. By eight o'clock, he felt as if elephants were doing a jig in his stomach, and he could scarcely wait for Skip to give him the radio details of the game.

Skip dashed up the steps to the office to tell him that Freeman was tuned in all right and that Assembly Hall was jamming. After the first ten minutes, Skip reported that State was leading by four points. "They're ahead 25-21, Chip! What do you think of that?"

It was the same ten minutes into the second half. The Statesmen were still out in front, 67-63. Chip couldn't take it. He had to do something and began a random tour of the store, spending as much time as possible at each counter, but he avoided the stockroom. Finally, when he couldn't stand the tension anymore, he went back upstairs to the office.

With the end of the game only minutes away, Chip began to pace back and forth, back and forth. Then he heard Skip's slow and lagging footsteps on the stairs, and he knew his teammates had lost.

Skip paused in the doorway. "No go, Chip," he said gloomily. "They killed us in the last five minutes."

"What was the score?"

"Eighty-nine to eighty. We were leading right up to the last five minutes. When they put on a press, we were dead and couldn't stop them."

Skip left and Chip remained at the desk until Soapy showed up to help close the store. The redhead didn't want to talk about the game, and Chip respected his wishes and left him to his thoughts. When they got to Jeff, Soapy went to bed directly after preparing Chip's bedtime snack. Chip was disheartened and tired. It had been a disastrous week.

CHAPTER 15

Victory for Sisyphus

SUNDAY MORNING, Chip got up at eight o'clock, showered and dressed, and walked over to the window to watch for Soapy. A little later he saw the redhead trudging slowly along the walkway in front of Jeff carrying a small grocery bag. Every few steps, Soapy would kick at a piece of ice or a clump of snow along his path. Soapy was way down. It was evident in his slow pace and slouched shoulders.

A few minutes later the redhead fumbled with the doorknob and entered the room. He tossed the papers on Chip's bed. "I think you'll be interested in some of the news," he said pointedly.

"About the game?"

Soapy shrugged. "That and some other things."

"What other things? Oh, I didn't think about it last night. Did you get in the game?"

Soapy's laugh was hollow and bitter. "Me?" he demanded. "Are you kidding?"

"How about Speed?"

"Speed didn't play either. Stone started Dom, Rudy, Branch, Jimmy, and J. C. Tucker, and that was it."

"No substitutions at all?"

"Not a one."

Soapy walked over to Chip's bed and picked up the *News*. It was opened to the sports pages, and Soapy spread it on the desk. "Come here."

Chip walked over to the desk and stood beside Soapy. "There," the redhead said, pointing to Jim Locke's column. "Read that!"

HOOP SENSE AND NONSENSE
by Jim Locke

Every seat in Assembly Hall was filled last night when the hometown Statesmen and the A & M Aggies squared off for a vital conference contest.

A & M ran away from State minutes before the buzzer to win the bitterly fought game by nine points with a score of 89-80. It was A & M's fourteenth conference victory in fifteen starts and State's third loss in thirteen league outings. Chip Hilton is still out of basketball action and may remain there for the balance of the season.

"That's what *he* thinks," Chip muttered.

"Read on," Soapy urged.

The loss to A & M last night virtually eliminated State from the conference race. To concede the Statesmen even a chance to overhaul A & M or Northern State at this stage of the season would be comparable to predicting victory for Sisyphus.

"Who's this guy Sisyphus?" Soapy demanded.

"I don't know."

"Well, what do you think of what he has to say?"

"I think he's out of his mind. We haven't been eliminated yet."

"Read the predictions," Soapy said, pointing to the next paragraph.

NEXT WEEK'S HOOP PREDICTIONS

Western—Away—Wednesday, February 22. State defeated Western here on January 14 by a score of 79-76. But the upcoming match is on Western's home court where they are almost impossible to beat. Further, Chip Hilton played in the first game, and without him, State is just another ball club. . . . Western by 10 points.

Northern State—Away—Saturday, February 25. Northern defeated State in the Holiday Invitational Tournament, 83-81. Hilton got 46 points in that game. Northern State lost to mighty Southwestern in the finals of the tournament. Coach Stone has more than one reason for hoping for a victory over his alma mater, but he will have to forego it for another year. . . . Northern State by 15 points.

"We'll see about that!" Chip said hotly. He crumpled the paper and threw it on the bed.

"Hold everything," Soapy said, retrieving the paper and smoothing it out. "There's more."

Chip turned back and continued with the column.

STATE CAMPUS GOSSIP

Campus gossip has it that the players are not sold on the slow-down control game (who is?) Coach Mike Stone has introduced . . . .

MORE CAMPUS GOSSIP

Reliable informants indicate that the Statesmen not only dislike possession ball but also resent some of the coaching methods of their new mentor, maybe to the extent of an organized rebellion. . . .

Chip finished the last paragraph and looked at Soapy incredulously. "Of all the junk Locke ever wrote," he said angrily, "this is the worst. *Organized rebellion!* That sounds like something out of a history book on the French Revolution, not the sports pages! The whole thing is ridiculous."

"It isn't all ridiculous," Soapy remonstrated. "None of the guys go for control ball. You don't either."

"That's right, Soapy, but we haven't given it a fair chance. How do we know whether or not it's the right offense for us?" Chip was angry through and through. "State players don't quit, and they don't start rebellions."

Soapy backed up. "Hold everything," he said, raising his hands to fend off Chip's onslaught. "I'm not saying Locke is right or wrong."

"I *am!*" Chip declared. "He's wrong and this rebellion foolishness is wrong. I'll get off this ludicrous ex-athletics list tomorrow and straighten out Di Santis and Slater and the rest of them, and I'll straighten Locke out too!"

"You really think Doc Terring will give you the OK tomorrow?" Soapy asked.

"Yes, I do!" Chip said angrily. "I've had enough of this nonsense." He eyed Soapy searchingly. "Are you sure you don't know anything about this rebellion deal?"

"Well, it hasn't reached the rebellion stage," Soapy said softly, "but some of the guys are pretty upset."

"They'll be good and upset when I find out who they are," Chip threatened.

"Did you see the conference standings?" Soapy asked.

"No, but I know what they are. I know another thing. I've heard enough of this possession alibi. A good team can use *any* offense and win."

"I know, I know," Soapy said hastily. "The way you're talking, I'd believe anything you say."

"All right. I'm going to church. You coming?"

"I sure am," Soapy promised. "The mood you're in, I'm not going to let you out of my sight."

Chip picked up his Bible and headed out the door with Soapy following closely behind. As the two friends walked briskly through town, Chip replayed Jim Locke's column in his mind. Sensing Chip's need to organize his thoughts, Soapy remained silent during the short walk to church.

As Chip and Soapy settled into their favorite pew, Pastor Potts welcomed the congregation to the morning service. Chip relaxed and released Locke's column and his teammates' attitudes from his mind. His thoughts returned to Valley Falls and his mom. She had always told him that she believed things work out the way they're supposed to—no matter how much we plan or worry. Chip knew she was right. He would do everything he could to make things right with the team and leave the rest to faith.

He caught Soapy watching him and gave his pal a smile to let him know he was OK. Soapy's wide grin in response made him thankful again for the strength of their friendship.

After church, they walked to Grayson's and opened the store. Soapy got busy at the fountain, and Chip picked up Freeman's order list and took it up to the office. A little later he heard someone ascending the stairs, but he didn't look up until a voice said, "Hello, Chip."

Chip sprang to his feet and rushed to the door. *"Mr. Grayson!"* Grasping his employer's hand, Chip shook it vigorously. Mrs. Grayson was right behind her husband, and Chip smiled and spoke to her also. Then he hurried to the desk and held the chair for his boss. "You look fine," he said. "Come on in and sit down."

"I feel fine," Grayson said. "Never mind the chair though. We're on our way home from the airport, but we had to stop in for a second to say hello."

"Chip," Mrs. Grayson began hesitantly, "I had to tell him about the basketball situation."

"You look all right to me," Grayson said. "How do you feel?"

"Fine, sir," Chip said. "I was staying up too late studying, but that's all over."

"That's what I understand," Grayson said dryly. "Now that I'm back on the job, I would like to see State University get back in the winning column." He paused and regarded Chip quizzically. "Do you think you can take care of that assignment?"

Chip nodded. "Yes, sir," he said. "Anyway, I can sure try."

"All right," Grayson said kindly. "I'll be on the job in the morning, and you go back to your old schedule. Mrs. Grayson and I are heading home now. I'll see you tomorrow after practice. But after that you're taking a few days off from here."

Chip walked out to their car with them and then hurried back to the office, taking the steps three at a time. "At last!" he cried in elation. "Basketball, here I come!"

The rest of the day passed quickly and smoothly, and when Chip went to bed that night, the urge to play basketball was so great that he tossed and turned for hours before going to sleep.

He couldn't get Locke's column out of his thoughts during his classes the next morning. When his last class was over, he headed for the student union and selected a cup of clear soup, a serving of chicken salad, *cold* milk, and squares of red and green Jell-o. Then he sat at the table where Dom and Rudy usually ate lunch. A few minutes later they came along, surprised to find him at their table.

"Hiya, Chip," Di Santis said, extending his hand. "How are you coming along?"

"Good."

"This is the big day, isn't it?" Slater asked.

Chip nodded. "It sure is."

"We've really missed you," Di Santis said. "It's been real rough without all those points you get for us."

"The points and a few other things," Slater added.

That gave Chip the opening he wanted, and he wasted no time in bringing up the subject of Locke's column. "What did you think of it?" he asked pointedly.

"I didn't like it," Di Santis replied. "Don't get me wrong, I don't like Stone a bit. But I never gave a thought to quitting or rebelling or planning a walkout or whatever Locke was trying to get at." He paused and regarded Chip carefully. "Did you really think we would do something like that?"

Chip sighed with relief. "No," he said slowly, "I didn't. I just had to find out, that's all."

"I'd like to get my hands on the guy who started that rumor," Di Santis said.

"That goes double for me," Slater added. "It was a dirty trick. I'm with Dom. I don't like Stone at all. But he *is* the coach. If he says hold the ball, well, as much as I dislike the idea, I say hold it. It's as simple as that."

Chip took the last bite of his chicken salad and carefully searched his teammates' faces. "How about the rest of the players?"

"How many more are there?" Slater asked. "Let's see, there's three of us here, and you know Soapy and Jimmy and Speed as well as anyone. So, who's left?"

"No one who would take the lead in that sort of a deal," Di Santis said.

"Look, Chip," Slater explained, "the guys have been doing a lot of griping. We were griping before you got sick, and it's gotten worse since we started to lose. But as for this rebellion business, we don't know anything about it. Even if there was something to it, we wouldn't do anything unless you knew about it. Right, Dom?"

Di Santis nodded. "That's for sure."

"That's all I wanted to know," Chip said, pushing back his chair. He lifted his tray, smiled, and nodded to his two teammates. "See you guys later." He paused and added, "It's all up to Doc Terring."

"Give it a big try," Di Santis encouraged.

"If Terring doesn't give you medical clearance," Slater added, shrugging his wide shoulders and spreading his hands, "we've had it."

"Not yet!" Chip said grimly.

He went to his next class and then struck out for Dr. Terring's office. He was half an hour early, but he waited quietly and confidently. Terring came in a few minutes before three o'clock and smiled at Chip's obvious determination. "Come in, Chip," he said heartily. "You look the best I've seen you in a long time."

"I *feel* the best I have in a long time," Chip retorted brightly.

"Well," Terring said calmly, picking Chip's card up from his desk, "let's find out."

The examination took only three or four minutes, but it seemed like an hour to Chip. He controlled his impatience, but it required every bit of will power he possessed.

"All right," Terring said at last, "put on your shirt."

"What about it, Doc?" Chip asked. "I never felt better in my life."

"Well," Terring said slowly, "your troubles are partly over. You—" Chip leaped to his feet and started for the door, but Terring called him back. "Wait a moment, young man. I'm not finished yet. You can go back to basketball, but only on a limited basis. I'll discuss that with the coach.

"And, Chip, I think you ought to know something. It might interest you to know that Coach Stone was the one who asked me to give you the examination."

It didn't register for a moment. Then Chip nodded. "You mean the first time? The first examination?"

Terring nodded. "Yes, it was his request."

"Well, what do you know," Chip said slowly. "I never gave him a thought."

"He gave you quite a bit of thought," Terring said gently. "I don't imagine you know much about the treatment he got from his old coach."

"No, I don't."

"Well, it was pretty rough. His greatest ambition has been to beat Northern State ever since. And," Terring added significantly, "without you, he didn't have a chance in the world to do it. But that didn't stop him from talking to me about your health.

"Well, young man, if you don't get a move on, you'll be late for practice."

CHAPTER 16

Joys
of Amateurism

JIM LOCKE looked up in surprise and then laid the paper he was reading on his battered metal desk. "Hello, Hilton," he said, quickly rising to his feet and extending a hand. "Just reading what I wrote about you in my column. How did it feel to get back in uniform?"

Without waiting for Chip to reply, he continued, "From what I hear, your teammates put on quite a celebration when you barged into the locker room last night."

"It felt pretty good," Chip said.

"Sit down," Locke said, gesturing toward the chair beside the desk. He sized Chip up for a moment. "You look fine," he continued warmly. "Did you lose your shooting eye?"

"Not quite," Chip said, "but I wasn't very sharp."

"Knowing you," Locke said, grinning, "I'm sure you didn't like what I wrote about Sisyphus in Sunday's paper. Right?"

Chip laughed. "Well, frankly, I had to look him up to find out what the allusion meant, to find out he was a hopeless figure in Greek mythology. I don't agree that we're out of the conference race, but that isn't what I came to see you about."

"The player rebellion," Locke suggested, eyeing Chip keenly.

"That's it," Chip said, nodding.

"All right, what's the story?"

"It isn't true."

"Are you trying to tell me that you and Di Santis and Slater go for Stone's control game?"

"I don't mean that. I mean there is no truth to the rebellion part of the story."

Locke studied Chip for a long moment and then nodded as if in reflection. "So that's it. You're nipping it in the bud."

"I—"

"Never mind, never mind," Locke said hastily. "I know what you're trying to say. All right," he said decisively. "If you say it was a mistake, I'll go along and I think I can fix things. Take a look at tomorrow's column."

"I won't get a chance to see it until Thursday," Chip said. "We're leaving for Western the first thing in the morning. I would appreciate it if you kept my name out of this."

Locke waved his hand airily. "It's nothing, Hilton. By the way, how do you feel about tomorrow's game?"

"We're going to win."

"What makes you so sure?"

"I'm just sure," Chip said firmly.

"How about Northern State?"

"We'll win that one too."

"I wish you success," Locke said, "but I have to be practical. You haven't got a chance to win on their court. They lose a game at home only on an average of once in five years."

"Then this is the year," Chip said stubbornly. "And we'll be the team to make it happen. We've got a little score to settle with Northern State."

Jim Locke smiled and nodded his head thoughtfully. "This is all right," he said. "You've got a feud going with the Northern State players, and Stone's got one going with Brannon. Sounds like a good story."

"I don't know how Coach Stone feels, but the rest of us would rather win that game than any other on the schedule."

"Well, Hilton, I'd like to see you do it, but all I can see is Sisyphus and his stone. You'll never do it."

Locke rose to his feet and thrust out his hand. "Anyway, Hilton, I admire your spirit. Nothing would make me happier than to be wrong about my predictions. I *will* say I think State would have won the conference if you hadn't gotten sick and couldn't play. I *know* you would have won the national scoring title. Now Kinser seems to have it locked up."

"How about Henninger?"

"I don't think he can catch Kinser." Locke snapped his fingers. "Oh, yes, I knew there was something I wanted to tell you. There's a better than even chance you can land the best national shooting average. Well, once more, good luck."

They shook hands, and Chip walked away. When he reached the street, he headed out in a jog for Assembly Hall. Now, to get the guys fired up for the game with Western. . . .

The next night, in Western University's modern field house, Chip leaned forward with his elbows on his knees and stared at the floor. He was lacing and unlacing his fingers, testing and loosening them up, trying to bring back the sensitivity and feel that had been all but lost in his enforced lay-off. Beyond the walls of the locker room he could hear the shouts of the players competing in the preliminary game, the shrill tone of an official's whistle, and the scattered cheers and yells of the Western fans.

It wouldn't be long, he was thinking, until he would know whether or not he still had the touch. Practice shooting and game shooting were as different as day and night. He remembered the last game with the Westerners all too well. Mike Stone had been trying to teach the Statesmen his control game and, between the halves, had bawled them out for lapsing back into their run-and-shoot game. Quitters, he had called them. An open break had been so close that even now it gave Chip the chills to think about it.

He remembered, too, how he had lost confidence in his shooting. It had been a wild game, and the score had been tied with less than a minute to play. One of his teammates had passed the ball to him, and he'd had an open shot yet been afraid to shoot for fear he would miss. Maybe, he was thinking, it had been a blessing in disguise. Anyway, he had driven in for the three-point play, the narrow margin of victory.

Most of all he remembered how Mike Stone had talked to them after the game. The coach had explained that he thought it was necessary to ride them in order to wake them up and make them fight. A lot of things had happened since that game. Like the incident last night in the locker room after practice. He could still see the grudging respect in the eyes of Soapy, Speed, Dom, Rudy, Branch, Jimmy, and the rest of the Statesmen when he told them about Stone's part in the ex-athletics decision.

Well, Chip reflected grimly, Mike Stone wouldn't have to make them fight tonight. A man *had* to fight when his back was against the wall.

"All right, men," Stone said.

Chip had been so engrossed that he hadn't heard Stone call for attention, but something penetrated his thoughts and he glanced up to find his teammates all looking at him. Then he realized that it was the second time Stone had spoken.

"I guess you don't need a pep talk for this one," Stone continued, "and I'm sure you know what you're up against. Let's go!"

The game was a battle from the opening whistle to the end of the game. Western was fighting for recognition in the conference and had accounted for one of Northern State's two losses. Tonight the Westerners were primed to knock State out of contention.

Chip could scarcely wait to take his first shot. He had been shooting well in the warm-up drills, but *they* didn't count. Phillips got the tap, and Dom pulled in the ball and flipped it to Jimmy. The little dribbler's opponent charged him, and when Jimmy pivoted away, he found himself in a double-team situation. The new opponent took the ball right out of Jimmy's hands and dribbled the length of the court to score. The Western fans practically tore down the field house.

Chip took the ball out of bounds; and when he turned back to the court, his opponent was leaping and waving his arms and yelling at the top of his voice, a veritable jumping jack. Chip managed to get the ball to Slater, but Rudy ran into the same trouble Jimmy had encountered.

He, too, was double-teamed, and the opponents tied up the ball. The official signaled a jump ball, checked the possession arrow, and pointed to the inbounding spot for Western. Rudy's opponent outran him and was all alone under the basket when a teammate hit him with the ball. He scored, and Chip called time.

The Statesmen huddled, and Stone sent Speed and Reardon to the scorers' table to report for Slater and Phillips. "Man-to-man press," he said crisply. "Hilton! You and Chung and Morris and Reardon handle the ball. Dom! You work around the ten-second line until we get the ball clear and then light out for the base line. That'll spread them out! Don't waste any time on out-of-bounds plays. Just get the ball inbounds fast and hustle across the ten-second line."

Stone turned and sat down on the bench, and a moment later Speed and Bitsy returned from the scorers' table and joined the three starters. Chip thrust his hand out for the team clasp, scarcely able to resist a grin. This was the Statesmen's game, the kind of basketball they loved. Stone had given them the green light.

"Now we go!" he hissed. "Everyone know what I mean?"

"And *how!*" Di Santis gritted through set teeth.

The Statesmen didn't catch up with Western until nearly halftime. Then the dazzling speed and scoring abilities of Jimmy, Bitsy, Speed, and Chip began to tell, and when the half ended, the Statesmen were out in front, 41-37.

Stone didn't have much to say during the halftime intermission, but he did warn them that Western would undoubtedly change their attack later in the game if their press didn't function. "Don't get upset if they try something unorthodox," he warned. "We can match anything they try. Keep hustling."

Western resumed the second half with the press, but Speed, Jimmy, Bitsy, and Chip scored repeatedly, and State gradually drew away. Midway through the second half, State led 74-67. Then, in the last ten minutes of the game, just as Stone had predicted, Western called for a time-out and came back on the court in a double pivot offense. Now the opponents pounded their offensive backboard and began to pull up their score.

Coach Stone called time and sent Phillips and Slater in for Speed and Bitsy. "Use your control game now," he said calmly.

The Statesmen held the ball and screened and screened, waiting for the sure shot. And gradually the Statesmen again pulled steadily away from Western. When the buzzer sounded, State was an easy winner. The final score: State 88, Western 76.

It was a big win, and the players celebrated wildly in the locker room until Kelly reminded them they had less than half an hour to board the bus to the airport for their flight home. They were all business then, showering, dressing, and organizing their gear. They were an organized, disciplined, victorious team, and they were going home!

They arrived home late that night and were back in their regular routine the next morning, but with the game at Northern State only two days away, it was no time to start cheering.

Chip went to his classes and then joined Dom, Rudy, and Speed in the cafeteria at the student union. Soapy showed up a few minutes later with a copy of the *News*. He couldn't wait to show it to Chip.

"It's all about the game," the redhead said gleefully, handing the paper to Chip. "Did you know you got thirty-seven points?"

Chip shook his head. "Nope."

"Well, you did. And take a look at Jim Locke's column."

Chip quickly turned the pages to Jim Locke's column. He scanned the lines first for some sign of his name and breathed a sigh of relief when he saw it was not mentioned.

> Longtime readers will know I've been wrong on many counts in this column in the past and will undoubtedly be in error many times in the future. And, as has been the case in the past when mistakes occur, I hasten to make the necessary correction.
>
> Last Sunday morning, I gave credence to a State campus rumor that certain State cagers were organizing a rebellion against Coach Mike Stone to protest his coaching methods and style of play.
>
> The rumor has been scotched and discredited by a person who will remain unnamed but who would be the first to know of such a possibility. Once again, a campus rumor lacks the legs to stand up under scrutiny, and is this reporter's face red!

"Well?" Soapy said.

"It's about time," Dom rasped.

"Right!" Rudy added.

"Wonder who the last paragraph refers to?" Speed asked.

Soapy's eyes flashed from Speed to Chip and back again. "Got me," he said quickly.

"I know one thing," Dom commented. "We can thank the coach's possession game for part of last night's win."

"That's right," Chip added. "Stone's control game and Corrigan's run-and-shoot style make a pretty good combination." Chip lifted his wrist to check the time on his watch. "Well, guys, I've got a class. See you all at practice."

Coach Stone was as nervous as a cat during practice on Thursday and Friday. He reviewed the details of their offenses and defenses and drove them as though there had never been a Western game. He made no reference to the win and, as far as Chip could tell, he knew nothing about either of the columns Jim Locke had written.

The players gave their best. They tried hard to please Stone and put out every second. They wanted to beat Northern State as badly as he did, but they couldn't satisfy him. When he called an end to practice Friday night, the players' nerves were stretched too thin.

Soapy was dressed and busy packing his carry-on bag when Chip woke up the next morning. "Shirts, socks, underwear, sweats, tie, and shaving kit," the redhead recited. "I'm all set, Chipper. Good thing you packed last night. We have to be at Assembly Hall in a half-hour!"

A half-hour into their flight, Chip, Soapy, Speed, and Jimmy were sitting together in a center row, with Chip in the aisle seat. Speed was already engrossed in the latest edition of *Sports Illustrated,* and Soapy and Jimmy were listening to their Walkmans. After the meal, Chip was just dozing off when student trainer Andre Gilbert walked down the aisle and tapped him on the shoulder. "Coach wants to talk with you for a minute, Chip," Andre said, gesturing to a seat about ten rows in front of them.

Stone, sitting in a window seat, had his tray table down and was studying the Northern State scouting notes. He motioned to the empty seat next to him. "Sit down, Hilton," he said. "I'm just going over the scouting notes again. I don't want to overlook anything." He studied Chip for a second. "Feel all right?"

"Fine, Coach."

"I hear your boss is back. Is that going to make it a little easier on you?"

"A lot easier, Coach. I'm back on my old schedule now."

Stone leaned back in his seat and slowly exhaled. "Beats me," he said, shaking his head thoughtfully. "I've never met an athlete like you in my whole life. And I've met a lot of them. *All* of the good ones and most of the great ones want *everything.* Room, board, books, the works! Some of them want more. And," he continued, "some of them get more, one way or another. You're so different it hurts. You don't want *anything.*"

Stone paused and looked at Chip expectantly, but the star had nothing to say; he had said it all before.

"Well," Stone said at last, "let's review our plans for tonight."

They went over the Northern State offense and defense, each player's moves and weaknesses, and the player match-ups. The time passed quickly, and they were still engrossed in the scouting notes when the flight attendant announced the plane was on its final approach. Mike Stone placed the scouting notes in a portfolio, stowed his tray table, and turned to Chip. "This has been a long session and I know you're tired, but there was something I didn't cover."

"What's that, Coach?"

"Jim Locke's column in the *News.* I read it last Sunday and also on Thursday."

"The whole thing was an exaggeration, Coach."

Stone smiled. "Could be," he said. "Anyway, I understand that's what you told Locke."

CHAPTER 17

Battle of Mistakes

CHIP GLANCED at his coach in surprise. "Then you knew! You knew all the time."

Stone nodded and smiled. "Yes, I did. And I think there are a few things you should know. First, I've been doing a lot of thinking since I learned how you went to bat for me. And I think I owe you, as the captain of the team, some sort of an explanation."

Chip started to protest, but Stone stopped him. "This will only take a minute or two, and perhaps it will enable you to put yourself in my place.

"You know, of course, that I played and coached at Northern State. Like you, I love my alma mater, and I always will. My greatest ambition as a player was to coach at Northern State after graduation.

"Well, to make a long story short, I got the job as the head assistant to Coach Brannon as soon as I graduated. I was thrilled. Coach Brannon is the head basketball coach and used to be the athletic director at Northern State. He's been there a long time. Practically an institution himself, you might say.

"Anyway, I played for him, and he's plenty tough. I was his number-one assistant for seven years, and I guess most of his methods rubbed off on me. Anyway, everyone figured I would be his successor, and that was my big dream."

Mike Stone paused and cleared his throat before he continued.

"I wanted to be head coach of my alma mater so badly that it hurts even now to think about it. At any rate, Coach Brannon's son, Bob, graduated from Northern State last June, and at the beginning of the year, the coach gave Bob my job as the head assistant coach. I lost most of my responsibilities. That hurt.

"The coach gave the excuse that I was a good teacher of fundamentals and could help him more by working with some of our incoming freshmen. Of course, he didn't say anything then about his retirement coming up the year after next. That's why I wanted the State University job so much. It would have been hard to swallow being there when Bob becomes head coach."

"Did his son play varsity?" Chip asked.

"He wasn't a starter, but he got into some games. Anyway, to get back to the coach and myself, all my respect for him turned to a desire for revenge. I wanted to get even with him more than anything else in the world. The best way I could dream of evening up the score was to take a team up there and beat him on his home court.

"And ever since I got the job at State, I haven't been able to think about anything else. Everything I have taught you players and every practice session has been directed toward getting State University ready to beat Coach Brannon."

Stone paused and shook his head wryly. "Hate is a dangerous emotion, Hilton. It poisons your mind and eats at you until it becomes your whole world.

"Well, I was so wrapped up in my desire for revenge that I forgot all about you players. Looking back, I can see that I had forgotten how the players felt even when I was Coach Brannon's assistant.

"Brannon runs a tough scholarship policy. His basketball players earn everything they get. He bears down on them all the time. They play the way he wants them to play—hard and rough and— Well, I started to say dirty but that's not quite right. Let's say they play to the hilt and just inside the rules.

"When Locke—"

"He always writes stuff like that, Coach," Chip interrupted.

Stone nodded. "Yes, I suppose so. Anyway, he gave me something to think about. Last Sunday's story had nothing to do with what I'm about to say. I just want you to know that you've taught me more about leadership and coaching in six weeks than Coach Brannon taught me in more than ten years.

"When I said I had never met an athlete like you, it was meant in admiration. It's too bad all athletes don't have your concept of amateurism and your determination to preserve it. You're a true amateur and play for the sheer love of the game. If others did, most college coaching jobs wouldn't depend so desperately on winning. Players make coaches, and in striving to get outstanding prospects, coaches have to engage in cutthroat competition. Some universities make all kinds of promises and inducements to land good players. I don't want to be like that. I want to be your coach."

"Coach, we're with you, all the way," Chip said earnestly. "Whether we win or lose, you're our coach. We respect you, and if we can, we'll win this game, for you."

"Thank you, Hilton," Stone said, visibly moved. "You better head back to your seat. It looks as if we're about to land."

Tension gripped every member of the State University basketball program in the locker room. Chip could almost feel the tension in the very air he breathed. His teammates were dressing deliberately and purposefully, and their short, terse answers to Kelly's questions told most of the story. They knew the bitter battle that lay ahead. Coach Stone was pacing back and forth near the door.

Murph Kelly had just finished taping Rudy Slater's ankle, and as he checked the rest of the Statesmen, his eyes shifted from one player to the next to make sure he and Andre had overlooked no one. "All right, Coach," he nodded grimly, his lips drawn tight and straight. "They're all set."

The players straightened up as Stone walked to the center of the room and began to speak. "I'm not one to go in for pregame locker-room speeches," he said, biting off the words, "but there are exceptions to every rule." He paused and moved a step closer.

"This is a big game for you. But perhaps it's an even bigger game for me. I am so anxious for you to win tonight that there just aren't enough words in my vocabulary to tell you how badly I want this victory. But that's personal, and I shouldn't even be thinking about it. Excuse me."

Stone turned, took a step or two away, and then pivoted back. "Northern is tough at anytime, but they'll be tougher tonight. They're playing on their own court in front of their home crowd, and that's a tremendous advantage. But their *big* incentive, like yours, is to win the conference title. A loss tonight would practically eliminate them. On the other side of the ledger, however, a win for you will keep State's hopes alive.

"The fans here are partisan and loud, and I mean loud. But you've played in Madison Square Garden, and the crowds there are pretty noisy, too, so the enthusiasm of the locals shouldn't bother you much.

"The officials sometimes call them a little different on this court. They permit more contact, particularly when the situation is away from the ball or not involved with a scoring play. You'll adjust to that easily enough, but I'm afraid Coach Brannon's antics may upset you a bit. He puts on quite a show. You must have noticed his performance in New York at the Garden—"

"We sure did!" Soapy muttered in a muffled voice.

"Strangely enough," Stone continued, "the officials often let Coach Brannon get away with a little more than some of the other coaches. I guess it's because he's an old-timer.

"Northern State is bigger than you are, and they play rough, real rough. They get away with it. But you are better passers and shooters. Coach Brannon has no one who can match Hilton, and that means Chip's going to be double-teamed and roughed up a bit. I wish he were in a little better shape."

Stone's voice softened. "A part of that is my fault, but we haven't time to discuss it right now."

There was a deep quiet in the room as Stone resumed his pacing. Then the silence was broken by a crowd roar that must have been tremendous, because it filtered clearly through the door and walls of the locker room. It had to mean the appearance of the home team on the court. Stone spun quickly around and checked his pacing. The spell was broken, and once more his voice was brisk and sharp. "We'll start with Hilton, Di Santis, Slater, Chung, and Phillips.

"One last word. This game will be a battle of mistakes. The team that makes the fewest will win. Let's go!"

Chip had never been gripped by a greater desire to win a game during his entire sports career. As soon as Stone tossed the ball to him, he dashed out of the locker room and led his teammates out onto the court and into a bedlam of crowd noise and flurried activity. Dribbling the ball under the basket, Chip made the layup and cut back to the center of the court to take his place in the warm-up drill.

The cries, shouts, and cheers of the crowd were loud and sustained, and mixed in were jeering yells of ridicule directed toward the Statesmen. Chip smiled grimly. Stone obviously knew what he was talking about. The coach's description of the fans hadn't been exaggerated.

Before the start of the game the Northern State players returned to their locker room. Stone motioned for the Statesmen to continue with their shooting. Five minutes later, just as the officials reached the scorers' table, the Northern players returned to the court.

The referee signaled for the captains, and Chip joined the Northern State leader and the officials in the center of the court. There were no unusual floor conditions to discuss, and the officials wished both captains well. Chip extended his hand to the Northern State captain, but he had turned quickly away.

A moment later the referee blasted his whistle, and the Statesmen joined hands with Stone in the usual team clasp. It was the fifteenth time the coach had been surrounded by Statesmen at the start of a game, but it was the first time the players had practically climbed over one another to grasp his hand.

The buzzer sounded, and the State starters walked out on the floor and began their usual maneuvering for positions. Chip figured Phillips could get the jump and gave the sign for a tap on the right side of the circle. The referee tossed up the ball, and the game was on.

Phillips got the tap, and Chip came in high and got his hands on the ball. But as he came down, two bulky Northern players crashed into him and knocked him roughly to the floor. It was an obvious foul. The ball flew out of Chip's hands and rolled out of bounds, but there was no whistle and Chip leaped to his feet, burning with anger.

Chip could hear Soapy shout something from the State bench, but his mind was focused on something else. Limping slightly, he backpedaled to a position opposite his opponent.

Chip leaned over a bit, rubbing his knee, apparently trying to recover from his fall. One of the Northern guards stepped out of bounds and passed the ball confidently toward Chip's opponent. But Chip had been playing possum!

He darted forward, intercepted the pass, dribbled the length of the court, and dropped the ball through the State basket for the first score of the game. The crowd roared, but it was more a roar of surprise than acclaim.

The Northern players were more careful now; they advanced slowly into the front court and set up their corner-to-corner roll. They were expert in this kind of basketball; it had been hammered into them since they had played as freshmen. Now, after a number of passes and much maneuvering, they established a perfect screen. But the player with the ball waited until a booming voice shouted, "Shoot!" Then he took the shot and scored.

The roar of the crowd had been continuous since the first tap, and it didn't let up as the Statesmen advanced to their front court. Chip and Jimmy started Stone's weave, only to find that Northern State was in a box-and-one defense. A Northerner was sticking to Chip, playing him close and crowding his every move on a man-to-man basis, while his four teammates were set up in a box zone near the basket.

Chip and his teammates continued the weave; but Slater made a bad pass, and a Northern opponent intercepted the ball. The fans stomped and applauded, and the crowd roar increased as the home players advanced slowly and started their roll. Again the booming voice gave instructions to the Northern players.

This time Chip located the source. It was Coach Brannon. He was standing up in front of the Northern State bench, his hands cupped to his mouth, shouting orders on almost every pass.

The tempo of the Northern offense never changed, and on the defense, their box-and-one stopped Stone's weave cold. The home team went out in front and steadily increased the lead until the score was doubled. After just ten minutes of play, Northern State led 18-9.

BUZZER BASKET

All through the half, Chip had heard Coach Brannon shouting instructions. It seemed impossible that his players could hear and understand him, but they did. Brannon would shout, "Shoot!" when a player had a clear shot and, "No!" when he didn't. When his team was on the defense, Brannon continued his shouts. And when a player made a mistake, the coach's shouts were angry and abusive.

Stone tried desperately to stop the slaughter. He used up two time-outs, and the Statesmen listened and tried to follow his instructions, but nothing worked. It was impossible to score with Stone's weave against the box-and-one, and the Northern University roll slowly but surely piled up the points.

The fans rode Stone unmercifully all through the half. "You shouldn't have left Northern, Stone!"

"Go home, Stone!"

"Once an assistant, always an assistant."

"Why don't you throw in the towel and quit?"

Brannon added to the show. When time was out, he stood outside his circle of players and watched Stone, grinning sarcastically while his former assistant talked. Chip and his teammates saw the by-play and it burned them up, but they couldn't do anything about it.

Just before the end of the half, Phillips made an interception, and Chip cut upcourt along the sideline in front of the Northern bench. Phillips saw him and threw a hard, straight pass. Just as Chip reached for the ball, a foot shot out from the Northern State bench, tripping him and sending him flying headlong. He sprawled flat on the floor and the ball flew out of bounds.

Although it had all happened in a split second, Chip had glimpsed a blue-trousered leg just as it was withdrawn after the contact.

He scrambled to his feet and looked back toward the Northern State bench. Coach Brannon was staring straight ahead, pretending he had seen nothing. The rest of the Northern players on the bench were dividing their attention between him and their coach. All of them convulsed with scornful laughter.

Chip forgot all about the game, the ball, the play, and his opponent. The fans sitting behind the bench had seen the tripping incident, and they joined in the laughter as Chip stood there, shaking with anger.

The official handed the ball to a Northern player standing on the sideline, and he inbounded the ball. Chip continued to stand there, looking straight at Coach Brannon. And he made no move even when his opponent took the incourt pass and scored.

Coach Stone had leaped up from the bench when Chip fell. Now he ran to Chip's side and took him by the arm. "That was a dirty trick, Brannon!" he cried.

Northern State's coach stood up and grinned contemptuously at his former assistant. "Aw, quit crying and take that fake all-American of yours back in front of your own bench. Can't you take a beating like a man?"

Now it took all of Chip's strength to restrain Stone. The tall giant's face was fiery red, and he was trembling with rage. "Sportsmanship!" he cried. "Brother!"

The State players came flying from their bench. They were met by the Northern State players in front of the scorers' table. Fortunately, the officials were on the job; they got between the two groups and managed to gain control.

Chip and Soapy led Coach Stone back to the bench, accompanied by the boos of the fans. "I've got to control myself," Stone said bitterly. "Just got to! Are you all right, Hilton?"

Chip nodded. "I'm all right."

The official blasted his whistle and carried the ball toward the Northern University end line. "State ball!" he cried. "Let's go!"

There was only enough time for the ball to be passed in-bounds before the buzzer ended the first half. The score: Northern State 43, State 18.

As Mike Stone walked with dignity off the court, the spectators bombarded him with caustic remarks and boos every step of the way. But he was cool and calm and kept his eyes straight ahead, apparently oblivious to the abuse.

Chip had been mauled and pushed and held by his opponent, but he had let it pass. Instead, he had concentrated on playing the game. But Coach Brannon's and the Northern University fans' poor sportsmanship was just too much. Now he was boiling with rage. He had to fight with himself to still the urge to lash out at the injustice of the entire situation.

The Statesmen followed their coach down the hall to their locker room. When they got inside, they threw themselves down on the benches, feeling frustrated and angry. But they kept quiet, rested, and waited. Murph Kelly took care of their injuries and checked ankles, and Andre Gilbert passed from player to player with sliced oranges. When five minutes had passed, Kelly looked at the coach and tapped his watch.

Stone took a deep breath and walked out in front of the players. "I'm a fool," he said simply.

CHAPTER 18

Tactical Changes

MURPH KELLY leaned slowly back against the trainers' table and stared at Coach Mike Stone in shocked surprise. Andre Gilbert stood as if transfixed. It was as if he were a figure captured on canvas, scarcely breathing as he held a basket of oranges just inches above the table. The players looked at Stone in wide-eyed amazement.

"I talked to your team captain on the flight," Stone continued, "and I tried to explain some of my actions to him. I've known Chip Hilton only a short time, but I know the kind of man he is. I know he said nothing to you about the personal part of our conversation. I want to take time right now to clear that up.

"I repeat, I'm a fool! First, I let my personal feelings interfere with my coaching. I was thinking about getting even with someone. I let that negative emotion blind me to my first responsibility—the welfare of my players. *You!*

"Second, because Coach Brannon gave away my job as his head assistant to his son and essentially demoted me, my pride was hurt, and I could think of nothing greater than coming back here and beating his team, *at his own game!* That was wrong because it was personal and had nothing to do with you.

"Third, I've been trying to force a style of play on you that takes years of practice and requires a particular kind of player. It was a grievous mistake. How stupid can one man be? I was wrong on all three counts. I'm ashamed, and I apologize."

Someone was hammering on the door and yelling, "Time to go! Second half!"

Stone acted as if he had not heard the interruption. With his head held high and his voice humble, he looked steadily from player to player. "So," he continued quietly, "it's my fault that you're down twenty-five points and are being humiliated by a team that can't carry your shoes. I've put you in a terrible hole, but that's done, and crying about it won't help."

There wasn't a sound and no one moved as Stone continued. "It isn't right for you to lose tonight. The display of poor sportsmanship to which you have just been subjected is, in itself, enough to arouse the same kind of feelings in your hearts that I had in mine. But that's no good. Those feelings do not, I repeat *do not,* belong in sports. Besides, you aren't that kind.

"Now, I believe you can still win this game. I know what you are made of and I know your captain. So," Stone paused to let the words register and then continued, "as of right now, we're going to drop our slowdown offense and go back to the attack Coach Corrigan taught you."

He looked around the circle of faces and said, "Hilton, who do you want to go back in there with you this half?"

Chip hadn't expected this. He thought for a moment and said, "We need points in a hurry, Coach. I'd like to start with Speed, Rudy, Bitsy, Jimmy, and myself and try the press. That's the same lineup we used against Mercer."

TACTICAL CHANGES

"All right!" Stone said decisively. "That's it! Now let's get out of here and run Coach Brannon and his team right off their own court. Come on! Let's do it!"

It was if everyone in that room had suddenly been swept upward by a giant tornado. The players leaped to their feet and yelled at the top of their voices less than a split second after Stone had finished the words.

Chip felt as if a tremendous weight had lifted from his chest, and he yelled and cheered as hard and as loud as the rest of them. He grabbed the practice ball off the table and dashed for the door with his teammates right behind him. They ran through the door, up along the hall, and out on the court. The Statesmen were yelling and cheering as if they had just won the game instead of being twenty-five points down.

The fans seated on all sides of the field house couldn't understand it and looked at one another incredulously. What was wrong with these State University players? Didn't they know the score? The spectators glanced at the scoreboard to make sure. This was different! Or crazy! Or something!

The referee blasted his whistle. He, too, looked bewildered. The home team was shocked and massed in front of their bench. The Northern State cheerleaders froze mid-chant and stared at the State University basketball team as if they were all out of their minds.

The Statesmen filed over to their bench. As the cheerleaders led a routine out on the floor, the fans joined in the Northern State University cheer. But all the spectators kept their eyes focused on the visiting players. They watched in utter amazement as Chip, Soapy, Speed, Bitsy, Rudy, Dom, and the rest of the guys continued to shout and cheer even while they were standing in front of their bench.

The Northern State players weren't listening to Brannon. Instead, they were looking at the Statesmen, staring curiously, perplexed by the strange display of enthusiasm. Had their visitors gone mad?

The Statesmen crowded around Coach Mike Stone and fought to get through the circle to join in the team hand clasp. This was their coach!

And when the starting five ran out on the floor, accompanied by the cheers of their teammates, the Northern State University players, coaches, and fans remained befuddled by the Statesmen's actions.

But Northern's befuddlement was just beginning! The State players who strode out on the court to line up against the home team looked more like high school players as far as size was concerned. When Northern State inbounded the ball, Chip surprised every person in the building by deftly cutting in front of his opponent to intercept it.

Speed came in sure and swift and took the ball from Chip. He drove hard and close to the floor and ducked under the two Northerners who tried to sandwich him as they had Chip at the beginning of the game. Chip had cut for the basket as soon as he was sure Speed had the ball. He easily outdistanced his opponent, and Speed zipped the ball to him just as he crossed the free-throw line.

Chip took his one-two, leaped up in the air, and dunked the ball with a foot to spare. It wasn't a showoff play; he had taken the shot without thinking. It was just an expression of his desire and joy and determination, and perhaps to show a bit of the uncontrollable disdain he felt for the Northern State University coach, team, and fans.

The Statesmen pressed as soon as the ball went through the basket. Jimmy and Bitsy trapped the receiver of the pass-in, and when he attempted to pass over them, Chip again intercepted the ball and drove in for the basket. A home-team guard tried to cut him off, but Chip went around him as if he weren't even there and dunked the ball once more.

One of the Northern State guards took the ball out of bounds under his basket and found himself looking at a jumping jack on a string. An energized Rudy Slater was leaping, yelling, waving his hands, and kicking his feet! When the guard threw the ball over Slater's head, Jimmy came from nowhere, leaped up, made the interception, and drove in for another score.

The same guard took the ball out of bounds again, and now it was Speed who waved his arms and kicked and yelled. This time the guard bounced the ball between Speed's legs, and Bitsy came tearing in, took the ball right out of the hands of the guard, and laid it up for the Statesmen's fourth basket in less than a minute. Coach Brannon had been on his feet yelling at the top of his lungs, and now the Northern captain finally heard him and called for a time-out.

Chip glanced at the scoreboard as he walked toward the State University bench. They were only seventeen points down now. Soapy, Bitsy, and Speed were shaking their fists in the air and yelling, but Coach Mike Stone just stood there and grinned at them, grateful admiration in his eyes. Then time was in. The Statesmen took up where they had left off; they stuck to their opponents like hound dogs on a rabbit scent and pressed constantly. They were trying for interceptions, taking chances, and attempting double-team plays.

The Northern State University fans were screaming, yelling, stomping, and pleading for their team to get organized. It was pandemonium.

When the Northern players did get the ball safely into their front court, they ran into another surprise. No longer was State in a man-to-man defense. One time they were using the switching defense, trading opponents every time Northern crossed; the next time they pressed at the ten-second line; and occasionally they zoned and double-teamed. And it was paying off!

The home players hadn't scored a point yet, and State had put together a run of seventeen straight points. Northern couldn't buy a basket, and the Statesmen couldn't miss, and Coach Brannon was hysterically calling for another time-out.

Chip glanced gleefully at the scoreboard. They were eight points down, and there were thirteen minutes left to play in the game. The pugnacious fans were still directing their attack toward Stone and the Statesmen, but some of them had shifted their attention to Brannon and the Northern players. And all the fans glanced at the scoreboard from time to time to make sure it was true.

When the time-out ended, Northern played more carefully. They had their counter-press attack going, but they couldn't stop the Statesmen. The only thing that slowed Chip and his teammates down were the fouls. The hard, aggressive play of the Statesmen meant making contact, and as the score mounted, unfortunately, so did their fouls.

Rudy Slater went out on fouls with twelve minutes left to play. Then Jimmy and Bitsy fouled out in quick succession. Now most of the State speed was gone. Their press began to falter. Northern State began to take advantage of J. C. Tucker, Dom Di Santis, and sophomore Marty Freedman for their scores. State called for a time-out.

Chip looked long and hard at the clock. There were seven minutes left to play, and Northern State led by the slim margin of two points, 61-59. State was running out of press players, and it didn't look good. If they lost Speed . . . .

Stone was evidently thinking the same thing, because when time was in, he called for another time-out. Of course, the partisan crowd got on Stone again, but Chip sensed that the quality of their cries and yells had changed. Instead of the raucous, sarcastic jibes they had all heard earlier, a measure of fear—or was it respect?—had crept into their voices.

"What do you think, Chip?" Stone asked, frowning, in the huddle. "What do you think we should do?"

It was the first time Stone had ever called him Chip, and it threw him for a moment. He looked around the circle of faces and concentrated on the situation. Speed, Dom, J. C., Marty, and he had been in the game. He shook his head.

Dom, J. C., and Marty weren't fast enough to keep up the pressure on Northern. Some tactical changes were essential.

Coach Stone and Chip's teammates were looking at him, and he made the decision that had been working in the back of his mind since they had started the press. "Well," he said slowly, "I'd like to go back in with Dom, Speed, Branch, and Soapy and work our perimeter game. Soapy has a beautiful long shot, and he can get some easy baskets against the box-and-one."

Stone considered for a moment and then nodded. "Sounds good. Smith! Come here. Where are you?"

Soapy hurriedly elbowed his way through the circle of players. "What is it, Coach? Water? Towels?"

"I could use both," Stone said. "Aspirin too! But no, Soapy. I want you to report in for Tucker. Phillips! Go in for Freedman."

The timekeeper signaled the referee, and the official blew his whistle. But Stone called for yet another time-out. "We've got to be careful now," he said. "We might as well be sure we're all set."

When time was in, the rest of the Statesmen sat down and Stone extended his hand. "That was my last time-out, men," he said. "Be careful."

Soapy was looking down at the floor. The expression on his face was set, but his lips were moving almost imperceptibly, and Chip knew his best pal was saying a little prayer. This was the redhead's big chance!

Then the circle broke and they trotted out on the court.

It was State University's ball out of bounds, and Chip passed in to Dom and cut incourt. Northern State was still in the box-and-one, and he breathed a sigh of relief. Dom passed to Speed, and the ball went from Chip to Soapy to Speed and back to Chip. His guard stuck to him like a leech when he dribbled to the left side of the court, and the players in the box zone shifted in formation. Chip continued and set a screen in front of Soapy. Then he flipped the ball back over his shoulder and borrowed a page from Brannon's book. "Shoot, Soapy," he called. "Hit it!"

Chip held his breath when Soapy took the shot. He sighed in relief when the ball swished through the net to tie up the score. The crowd's roar wasn't for Soapy, but the redhead was grinning just the same as he backpedaled to his defensive position.

Soapy hit three straight times against Northern State's box-and-one, and his accuracy forced them to change to a straight man-to-man defense. Each time Soapy scored, however, Northern State came back with their possession offense and matched the tally.

With the score tied and the end of the game in sight, both teams were playing carefully, making sure of their passes and taking their time in meticulously setting up plays. Brannon was still yelling forlornly, but his voice wasn't as overwhelming as before, and Chip couldn't tell whether the boom had gone out of that voice or whether the crowd noise had finally succeeded in drowning out his bellows.

The teams traded baskets, and then Northern State recovered a fumble by Di Santis and scored. Northern State was ahead by two points with a minute left to play!

The fans went completely berserk. Speed Morris brought the ball swiftly downcourt and passed to Chip. Then the Statesmen tried desperately to shake someone free. But Northern State was fighting and playing tight, and the seconds ticked steadily away.

Soapy had moved to the right side of the court to his favorite spot, and Chip knew it had to be now or never. He dribbled between the redhead and his opponent and flipped the ball back to his pal. "Take it, Soapy."

Soapy didn't hesitate. He took the shot, and the ball zipped cleanly through the ring to tie the score once more, 70-70.

Chip glanced at the clock. Twenty seconds remained!

He backtracked and signaled Speed and Soapy. "Old seventy-seven," he said. "Remember?"

"And how!" said Soapy.

"Got it!" Speed added.

Northern State advanced slowly, and Chip waited near the center of the court. Speed was on his left, pointing to his opponent, and Soapy was on the opposite side in the first line of defense. All three were playing Valley Falls High School possum, retreating slowly, apparently exhausted and beaten. Behind them, near the basket, Dom and Branch waited grimly.

Northern State's playmaker dribbled slowly upcourt, glancing at the clock to make sure he got across the ten-second line within the prescribed ten seconds. He wasn't going to speed it up. There were only fifteen seconds left to play. He smiled confidently and dribbled on across the line.

Chip advanced slowly toward him, overshifting to force the dribbler toward his left. The playmaker grinned and slanted his dribble toward Speed, and Chip held his breath in exultation; the Northern player had taken the bait!

Chip waited a second longer and then suddenly yelled, *"Now!"*

He charged the startled Northern player, who took his eyes off Speed for just a second, but it was enough!

Speed Morris sprang forward and made a slap at the ball. He got a piece of it, and it went spinning back over the line, with Chip madly in pursuit. He scooped the ball up and dribbled hard for the basket. Soapy's guard caught up with Chip, and the two ran side by side toward the State University basket. Chip could see Soapy cutting down the right sideline, but he continued the dribble, holding his breath, expecting to hear the buzzer on every bounce of the ball.

Chip could have forced the shot, but he remembered one of Coach Corrigan's old passing axioms: *Look down and pass high or look up and pass low.*

BUZZER BASKET

Without slackening his lightning-fast drive, he looked up at the basket and then flipped the ball down and around the Northern opponent to Soapy just as the redhead drove under the basket.

Soapy gathered in the ball and sweetly laid it against the backboard just before the buzzer sounded to end the game. The ball spun once around the ring, hesitated as if to tease everyone, and then dropped through the basket.

Chip turned and looked at the scoreboard. The big lights flickered twice. There it was: Visitors 72, Home 70.

The fans couldn't believe it. It couldn't happen! Not by *this* team! Not by *this* coach! Not in *this* game! State University had been down by twenty-five at the half!

Chip and his pals looked at the scoreboard to make sure. There it was, as tall as a man, in lights, and forever registered in the collegiate records.

Visitors 72, Home 70.

The fans looked back down on the court and saw the jubilant visitors gang up on their new coach. They lifted him up on their shoulders and carried him around the court. They were still yelling, just as they had yelled when they came out on the court at the start of the second half!

It wasn't any use to look for the Northern State coach. The old master had left as soon as the buzzer sounded. It was hard to believe, but he hadn't even stopped to argue with the officials. He was gone . . . and something had gone out of the fans.

Perhaps it was shame they felt for the poor sportsmanship shown by some of the hometown supporters, or perhaps it was the real sportsmanship that was there all along but which had come to the surface because of the play and fight of the visiting athletes.

Whatever it was, the cheers started faintly and grew in volume until they were one giant roar as the Northern State fans watched the Statesmen carry their coach off the court and out of sight.

CHAPTER 19

Comeback Victory

IT WAS a great victory for the State University Statesmen, and the visitors' locker-room celebration was something to witness! Chip and his teammates were enjoying one of the greatest thrills in sports, a comeback victory against overwhelming odds.

While the players were letting off steam, an overwhelmed Coach Mike Stone sat on Murph Kelly's trainers' table repeating over and over. "You did it! You did it! You were great! Absolutely great! The greatest basketball team I've ever seen on the collegiate court!"

Soapy Smith and Andre Gilbert were leaning over the scorebook, conspiratorially checking the game totals. "We made fifty-four points in the last half," Soapy yelled excitedly. "How about that!"

"While they were making twenty-seven," student manager Andre Gilbert added. "Chip! You got forty-one points!"

"Hold it! Hold everything!" Soapy interrupted. "Let me check one last item. Here! Gimme that book! Ahem. Now listen, everybody! Hey! Listen up! State's scoring prodigy, the go-go kid himself, the great Soapy Smith, pulled the game out of the fire with—let me see now, oh, yes, fourteen, now get this—*fourteen clutch points.*

"*And,* now hold it. The great Smith scored the two most important points, the last two, because *they* nailed the coffin lid on old man Brannon and his Northerners and dumped them into the grave of—yes, the grave of—despair."

Soapy hurled the book up into the air and leaped on the table. "Yippee!" he yelled. "Let's have three cheers for our coach! Come on, now!"

"Rah, Mike! Rah, Stone! Rah Coach Stone!"

Soapy leaped down, and he and the gang hoisted Stone up on the table. "Speech!" they yelled. "Speech!"

Murph Kelly didn't have to yell for silence now. Coach Mike Stone looked down at the faces of his players, and he gulped and tried to clear his throat. But he couldn't do it, so he stood there, blinking away tears. Finally the words came.

"This is the proudest moment of my life," he said slowly and earnestly. "I can't begin to tell you what it meant to me a moment ago when I listened to that cheer.

"My approach to coaching, in fact to my entire life, has been wholly wrapped up in basketball, in winning in basketball. I never gave a thought to the greater responsibilities of a coach. Now I realize the great opportunities coaching provides for guidance and leadership.

"I realize that the big challenge for a coach lies in choosing between a fanatical urge to win games or to dedicating his efforts to the leadership of his players, to their welfare and happiness. I know now that my approach was wrong. The big business side of basketball is the smallest part of coaching.

"I guess all that's left for me to say is that when my own son grows up and is lucky enough to make a team, I hope he has the opportunity to play with a bunch of great young men like you.

"Now this game is over and, yes, it was a wonderful victory. But it's only the beginning for you players. There is no limit to the heights you can reach in basketball or, more importantly, in life."

Stone started to step down from the table, but Chip sprang in front of him and held him back. Then he was the first of the Statesmen to look up at their coach and shake his hand.

Chip went back and sat down on the bench to take off his shoes. It had been great to win, especially this game. There were some tough games ahead before the season was over, but they were far away from Chip's thoughts. He was thinking back to the night of the Holiday Invitational. It had been only a little over two months ago that Coach Corrigan had said good-bye to the team and to State University basketball. Yet tonight it had seemed almost as if Jim Corrigan had been here, except that Mike Stone had been doing the talking.

Yes, Chip mused, he and his teammates had another Corrigan at last. They could truly go forward now, because they were a team again.

Afterword

WILLIAM "CHIP" HILTON has been my best friend since the seventh grade. I so vividly remember reading about Chip's world late into the night. I would get under the covers with a book and a flashlight, so I wouldn't disturb my family; and as I read, Chip's world would become my own world. As I fell asleep, I would dream of being on Chip's team. Those books transported me to Valley Falls, and there I was in the huddle with my idol and all of his friends. I was right there in the Hilton Athletic Club, with Chip barking out the play; and Soapy, Speed, and Fireball slapping me on the back. Thanks to reading, I developed a fabulous imagination. I was never bored on a rainy day when a Chip Hilton book was on the shelf.

Chip taught me many things. Through him, I learned not only how to attack a zone defense but, more importantly, how to attack and solve a pressing personal problem—how to face a crisis situation with inner strength, courage, and logical thinking. Chip and his pals showed me the importance of friendship. Not just having friends but being a friend was paramount. How gratifying it was to reach out and help someone in need, even at the expense of one's own interests. The man that Chip Hilton became through the years was highly respected and loved by all. I tried so hard to be just like him in my own life. No, I was never the guy who threw the touchdown pass or scored the buzzer basket. I did, however, develop a wonderful group of friends, and we have all gone through more than thirty years of enjoying one another's lives—sharing the joy of marriage and children and the sadness of death and difficult personal problems. Just like Chip and his friends, we teamed up to help each other through the tough times and celebrated the good times.

I have been a collector of the Chip Hilton Sports Series books all these years and have met hundreds of other Chip fans and collectors. Interestingly, we all share many of the same qualities. All of these people tell me the same thing: they wanted to be the type of person that Chip was. His moral character touched them, even more than his amazing athletic skills. We all found Chip to be respectful, polite, kindhearted, selfless, caring, and humble. What better role model could we have possibly asked for? The thrilling sports stories kept us interested in reading each book, but we all came away with so much more. Ultimately, author Coach Clair Bee built and shaped our development just as he had sculpted Chip's.

In real life, Clair Bee was very much like the Rockwell character in the books. His coaching record is as beyond belief as are Chip's heroics. How about a record of 222 wins and a mere 3 losses over a thirteen-year period! Coach Bee so believed in his moral lifestyle, and his Rockwell-like role as a mentor and teacher of young people, that he was devastated in 1951 by a point-shaving scandal that rocked not just his team but the whole college basketball world. He promptly resigned, not because he was involved or had any knowledge of this illegal activity. His own code of ethics applied to his personal life just as they applied to Chip's life, and because of this he simply felt that resignation was the only right thing to do.

AFTERWORD

I wish Coach Bee was still alive, so I could meet this great man, shake his hand, and thank him for the years of joy he has given all of us. For the life lessons he has taught us. For all the sports thrills he has shared with us. Since he is gone, I would like to extend those thanks to his lovely daughter Cindy and her husband Randy Farley. Thank you both for keeping your dad's dream alive—to share his wisdom with the future generations of young boys and girls. For persevering through the project of giving Chip Hilton a renaissance and introducing him to the new millennium. I hope everyone who reads the Chip Hilton books will share them with their friends and relatives and read them to their children. I'm sure they will instantly feel that William "Chip" Hilton is their best friend too! Happy reading!

Barry C. Hauser
Hollywood, Florida

Your Score Card

I have
read:

I expect
to read:

___ ___ 1. **Touchdown Pass:** The first story in the series introduces readers to William "Chip" Hilton and all his friends at Valley Falls High during an exciting football season.

___ ___ 2. **Championship Ball:** With a broken ankle and an unquenchable spirit, Chip wins the state basketball championship and an even greater victory over himself.

___ ___ 3. **Strike Three!:** In the hour of his team's greatest need, Chip Hilton takes to the mound and puts the Big Reds in line for all-state honors.

___ ___ 4. **Clutch Hitter!:** Chip's summer job at Mansfield Steel Company gives him a chance to play baseball on the famous Steelers team where he uses his head as well as his war club.

___ ___ 5. **A Pass and a Prayer:** Chip's last football season is a real challenge as conditions for the Big Reds deteriorate. Somehow he must keep them together for their coach.

BUZZER BASKET

YOUR SCORE CARD

BUZZER BASKET

I have I expect
read: to read:

_____   _____   19.*Backcourt Ace:* The State University basket-
                ball team has a real height problem, and the solu-
                tion may lie in seven-footer Branch Phillips. But
                there are complications. Be sure to read how Chip
                Hilton and his friends combine ingenuity and self-
                less service to solve a family's and the team's
                problems.

_____   _____   20.*Buzzer Basket:* State University's basketball
                team, sparked by Chip Hilton, seems headed for
                another victorious season. Then, in rapid succes-
                sion, a series of events threaten to obstruct State's
                great hopes. Chip Hilton faces some of his most
                serious challenges and tests of character in yet
                another book replete with friendship, personal
                courage, and Clair Bee's exciting basketball
                action.

About the Author

CLAIR BEE, who coached football, baseball, and basketball at the collegiate level, is considered one of the greatest basketball coaches of all time—both collegiate and professional. His winning percentage, 82.6, ranks first overall among major college coaches, past or present. His name lives on forever in numerous halls of fame. The Coach Clair Bee and Chip Hilton awards are presented annually at the Basketball Hall of Fame, honoring NCAA Division I college coaches and players for their commitment to education, personal character, and service to others on and off the court. Coach Clair Bee is the author of the twenty-four-volume, best-selling Chip Hilton Sports series, which has influenced many sports and literary notables, including best-selling author John Grisham.

CHIP HILTON MAKES A COMEBACK!

The Never-Before-Released *VOLUME 24* in the best-selling Chip Hilton series will be available soon!

Broadman & Holman Publishers has re-released the popular Chip Hilton Sports series that first began in 1948, and, over an ensuing twenty-year period, captivated the hearts and minds of young boys across the nation. The original 23-volume series sold more than 2 million copies and is credited by many for starting them on a lifelong love of sports. Sadly, the 24th volume was never released and millions of fans were left wondering what became of their hero Chip Hilton, the sports-loving boy.

Now, the never-before-released 24th volume in the series, titled *Fiery Fullback*, will be released in Fall 2002! See www.chiphilton.com for more details.

START COLLECTING YOUR COMPLETE CHIP HILTON SERIES TODAY!